THE LOST
DAUGHTER
COLLECTIVE

THE LOST DAUGHTER COLLECTIVE

A NOVEL

LINDSEY DRAGER

DZANC
BOOKS

DZANC BOOKS

5220 Dexter Ann Arbor Rd.
Ann Arbor, MI 48103
www.dzancbooks.org

Library of Congress Cataloging-in-Publication Data

Names: Drager, Lindsey, author.
Title: The lost daughter collective : a novel / Lindsey Drager.
Description: Ann Arbor, MI : Dzanc Books, [2017]
Identifiers: LCCN 2016031325 | ISBN 9781941088739 (paperback)
Subjects: LCSH: Fathers and daughters--Fiction | BISAC: FICTION / Literary.
Classification: LCC PS3604.R335 D73 2017 | DDC 813/.6--dc23
LC record available at https://lccn.loc.gov/2016031325

First US edition: March 2017
Interior design by Michelle Dotter

Printed in the United States of America

10   9   8   7   6   5   4   3   2   1

THE LOST
DAUGHTER
COLLECTIVE

PART I:

THE ROOM WITH TWO DOORS

No matter how dreary and grey our homes are, we people of flesh and blood would rather live there than in any other country, be it ever so beautiful. There is no place like home.

—*Dorothy*

It's no use going back to yesterday because I was a different person then.

—*Alice*

COME NIGHTS, THE GIRL crawls into bed to wait for her father to tell her a tale before sleep. He is down the hall working and she can just make out the sound of rapid typing from beyond his open office door. Because her room is one of the Institute's closets, converted into a child's private space, it is less a playground and more a chamber; the bookshelf also serves as a headboard and the door fails to open fully before hitting the foot of her bed.

At 1 a.m., the Scholar enters his daughter's room, where he finds her manipulating her hands to make shadows on the wall.

Good morning, young one, he says. *And happy birthday.*

The daughter drops her hands and folds them neatly over the cuff of her blankets. *Hello,* she says. That her father looks exhausted tells her that he is busy, but his efforts are spent on things other than her. She works to stay out of his way, but she cannot always contain her curiosity about the ideas over which he toils. She considers her own work the work of being his child. Is she a good daughter? But then, how can one know?

He speaks: *Because you are now five years old, the time has come to tell you a real story,* he says, running his hand through his greying hair. He walks to her form, which swells from beneath the too-small bed, sits on its edge. *A story about events that have come to pass, or what we call History. Do you feel ready for the truth?*

The girl reaches up to stroke her father's beard. It is rough between her tiny fingers and she thinks it feels the way a pet might. She collects as much hair as she can between the fingers of one hand and tugs. She squints to read what lies beyond his eyes, but learns nothing. She nods at him. He nods at her.

The Lost Daughter Collective gathers on the top floor of an abandoned umbrella factory in the downtown of a mid-sized city, he begins, and in beginning initiates The End. Down the hall, the men of the Wrist Institute will work through the night theorizing. In her room in the far east wing of the Institute, the girl will stay awake all night, too, having been installed with marvel that blossoms like blood from broken skin. For tonight is the first night she experiences what she will later understand as fear. And because fear is the bedmate of truth, it is tonight that the girl is inaugurated into her fifth year as well as the realm of history and horror.

Years later, he will publish the following in an introduction to the fifth edition of his seminal *The Myth of the Wrist*:

I have always believed that theory is not divorced from practice, but makes visible how all our experiences resonate and unite. As such, theory successfully illuminates the dark underpinnings of the human conundrum the same way art might. It is in this way that I hope my daughter's story can live on, not in celebration of her life and accomplishments, but as a cautionary tale for those who practice fatherhood. After all, if our stories are not relayed in the service of future generations, there is no reason to commit them to word. We do not tell our stories to share—we tell our stories to warn.

Her last letter to me was conveyed through a personal advertisement she took out in a paper she knew I read. Let this missive—directed from a sick girl to her sad father—be your first lesson in exploring the father-daughter paradigm:

My father is inside me by law, irrevocably, the same way there will always be laughter in slaughter.

THE LOST DAUGHTER COLLECTIVE gathers on the top floor of an abandoned umbrella factory in the downtown of a mid-sized city. The group is composed of men who meet weekly to harness their mourning, a delicate practice best not undertaken alone. Along with the roomful of fathers, there is weak tea and a healthy supply of biscuits neither sweet nor tart. A rich store of tissues is hidden in nooks throughout the large, single-room loft that composes the thirty-third floor, out of sight so as not to invite tears. Despite this, crying often ensues, though most of the men use their sleeves.

The fathers categorize their lost daughters in two ways: dead or missing. A dead daughter is deemed a Dorothy, a missing one an Alice. Qualifying their lost girls in this way is a silently endorsed coping mechanism. When a new father arrives, no one need articulate the method of daughter-exit from his life. The others can tell whether he is the victim of a Dorothy or an Alice by the new father's posture and gait. Father sorrow is best read through the mobile body.

Today one father—the plumber—has discovered his daughter is no longer an Alice, but a Dorothy. This is perhaps one of the hardest days for the father of an Alice, next to the day he learns she's become one and Daughter's Day.

The men take their seats, and the sound of folding-chair legs on the cement floor echoes through the empty loft. The chairs are arranged in a circle and the men change seats every week. Because they lead a life in which permanence reigns—a life where pink comforters lie disheveled in dusty bedrooms, where yellow hair ribbons and fruit-scented shampoo sit dormant on bathtub rims, where finger paintings of rainbows hang perpetually on refrigerator doors—they are only shyly acquainted with change and adopt it in meager kernels.

The leader of this troupe—the librarian—raises his eyes from his scuffed loafers to regard the plumber.

Do you want to start today?

The plumber looks out the window and scans the gray cityscape. *Fatherhood is an industry and a daughter is a beach,* he says, and a wave of gentle nods moves through the group. *But what binds them is cycle and scope. You can put the contracts in your suitcase—you can put the shells in your pocket—but you can't bring home the business or the shore.* All the men in the room look at the walls or their shoes.

In other words, it won't be easy to learn how to father a Dorothy, is that right? the librarian says, and the plumber purses his lips and makes a single jerk of his head such that his chin touches his chest, which they all read to mean *yes.* All the men who father an Alice breathe in deeply and sit back in their chairs, aware that they have lost one of their own, and aware that they too could become the father of a Dorothy. It is a possibility that, when it enters the father psyche, men everywhere carefully displace.

After the story is told, the plumber rises and the rest of the group follows, stretching and wiping their faces of tear, rubbing their temples and avoiding each other's gaze.

Because they know the night's work has only just begun, some men take advantage of the break. *Are the biscuits different this week?*

the real estate agent asks the landscaper, who shakes his head. *Must be my taste is returning,* the real estate agent says.

How long has it been? asks the bus driver.

Three years next Tuesday.

That's about right, the bus driver says and takes a swig of his tea. *Just know not to bother yourself with sweets.*

Sweets? the real estate agent asks.

Some cruel trick of the tongue, he says, and runs his hand over his white crew cut.

The men listen to each other's stories, a round robin arrangement where each gets the floor for twelve minutes. In those minutes, they share their cataloged tales of daughter-exit, here on the thirty-third floor of the abandoned umbrella factory—but too, across town in the attic of a church, the top floor of a library, the penthouse of a hotel. And too, across state lines and beyond the ends of the territory and even past the zones that designate time. And the stories travel across the weeks and months, across the years and beyond, carried and shared by voices to which the stories do not belong. In this way, the archive of daughter-exit is not shelved neatly, but rather casts a web over region and era, growing at an exponential rate. That the stories develop thus means both that the men have histories with which to anchor themselves, but also that girls exit every day, getting lost even now.

Each man holds the floor for twelve minutes to commemorate the age at which a girl-child becomes a young woman, a momentous event.

The narratives are told in several voices, by clans of men everywhere, simultaneously, until they become synchronized myth.

This is one attempt to share their story.

IN HER BOOK TITLED *On Departing and Apartment*, the woman who gave birth to the girl but whom was never called mother writes:

We cannot escape the place where from we come, for we move within invisible rooms with concealed walls that fail to break for door.

THE GIRL SPENDS THE first day of her fifth year in a haze, haunted by the threat of becoming lost. She roams the halls of the Wrist Institute seeking out the image of her father, who is shuttled between meetings and lectures. When he sees her in the hallways, she nods to him, and he nods to her.

The problem is this: when last night her father approached her, she had meant to ask him a question, but was put off by his immediate need to tell. What she now wants to share but finds herself struggling to reveal is that something is very wrong with her mouth. She had hoped to disclose this last night, but his mission seemed more important—to introduce her to the realm of the real. Before last night, she thought the event occurring in her mouth was a mere curiosity, but now, she thinks, absently working her hand to make shadows on the wide white wall, now all the facts of her life seem to harbor a secret. And suddenly her questions bear a certain heft. She is no longer concerned with how much ocean there is or from whence color comes because she realizes she knows so little about herself. For example, if her body can be lost, from where did her body derive?

The girl spends the afternoon in her room with the door shut and her lamp pointed coyly at the wall. She practices her shadow puppets and uses her tongue to investigate the occurrence in her mouth. The event can be explained quite simply: somehow, her teeth have become unfastened from her jaw. She thought at first it was one, but now a total of three seem to be free of their firm hold in her gums. She suspects this is punishment for saying an inappropriate word one afternoon in the cafeteria. She had called the asparagus *stupid*. Her father informed her that *stupid* was a blasphemous word that meant lazy, and when she had seen the asparagus hanging limply from her fork, she decided to test the word out since no one was there to hear. Certainly the event in her mouth is bound to this transgression. She assumes the teeth will resume their secure place if she discloses her crime, and as she wraps her hand in a towel in order to tilt the hot lamp, she decides this is what she will do tonight when her father comes. She will confess, and then apologize.

Years later, the girl will think of this day as one of her most bitter, but she will be wrong, for time will have cleanly amputated from her memory the other factor that overwhelmed the girl that day: it was the anniversary of her mother's going. Her father had told her when she was very young that her birthday was the same day as the day her mother left the circuit of the living. But this was all before the girl had come to understand the relationship between time and story, that one shifts the other such that fact grows soft and breaks apart.

At 1 a.m. her father enters, too quietly, and because her back is to the door, working to craft shadows on her wall, when he speaks, she flinches.

Good morning, young one, his voice booms. He looks down at his daughter whose face he shares and he thinks briefly of hearing the news that she would be. *Today I will tell you how the Lost Daughter Collective began. But now, how was your first day of age five?*

She takes a deep breath and sighs loudly. *I'm sorry*, she says.

My love, her father whispers, placing himself on the edge of her bed. He stretches himself to reach his face close to hers and they rub noses slightly, their private sign for love. *Never apologize for growing old.*

The girl looks at him with eyes so wide he can't decide if they harbor interest or fear.

I've not much time tonight, as we are preparing for the Wrist and Wing Convention, so let us begin. He clears his throat and adjusts his position on the bed, so that he does not look at her but at the blank wall and its blinding light. *The first meeting of the Lost Daughter Collective occurred when several fathers in the same village recognized their loss went beyond their capacity for coping alone.*

Years later she will pick up a copy of the only volume her parents co-wrote, *Doors and the Rhetoric of Permitted Entry.* A noted Room Scholar, her mother met her father at a conference concerning the intersections of flight and shelter. She will pick up the book and come to understand that her mother had written the story of her own end before she met it. The page reads:

> Most pregnant women attempt or succeed at suicide by hanging—this is to ensure, to some degree, the child contained within is preserved. Suicide while pregnant is a rare space to occupy, as the psycho-logic demonstrates contradiction: ushering in a new body without the outer body itself. Room Studies is engaged in this particular brand of death because of its investment in concentric spaces and methods of exit. Places are emptied following the Law of Water; masses of people collect and flee the same way water moves down a drain, first consolidating where exits exist, then waiting patiently until the rush of leaving en-

sues. What Room Studies finds compelling about this image is the damage humans will inflict on each other at the first cry of trauma—fire, for example, or a bomb—without confirming a threat exists. Building on the theories of Wrist and later Wing Scholars, it is our contention that the human psyche not only fears at some rudimentary place the notion of moving down, but also always seeks an out. Therefore, Room Studies contends that existence on earth is perceived as containment and the abstract everything-after is seen as escape.

When she is six, she will ask her father about the place from where she came, and he will tell her it was like a closet without windows, confined and lightless. *Like a prism in a storm*, he will tell her, but she'll hear *prison, swarm*.

THE FIRST MEETING OF the Lost Daughter Collective occurred when several fathers in the same village recognized their brand of grief as one that could not be shared with their spouses. It is said that the father-daughter relation is particularly complicated because the father does not harbor the daughter within the body as the mother does. That fathers do not carry within them their offspring means the relation between a daughter and a father is considered prosthetic.

The first fathers gathered and shared their tales, attempting through story to acquaint each other not only with the inner workings of their lost girls, but also with their private grieving methods for the phenomenon they would term daughter-exit. Their conversations extended, eventually, toward healing, and word of the underground, anonymous group's existence started traveling across the plains and mountains. In this way, the group grew; in the quake of their waves of loss, the seed of an idea was planted.

Those first fathers maintained their secrecy and anonymity, gaining membership through covert methods of invitation at the mourning ceremonies, whether grieving events or gatherings at governing structures to report their lost girls. To preserve their anonymity, the fathers identified themselves not by surname but occupation, a device that has persisted throughout the evolution of the Lost Daughter Collective even to its current iterations. The stories of these first fathers launched a rich catalog of narratives, a fractured and plural tragedy that emanates from the father body in complex ways.

The founding fathers include: The Barber, The Butcher, The Miller, The Woodsman, The Smith, The Angler, The Wainwright, and The Archivist.

THE GIRL WILL BECOME an ice sculptor. She will craft a theory called Cold Art Methodology and she will earn a position on the faculty of the Multiversity of the Mid-North. She will learn to cope with her childhood through harnessing and controlling light, then applying it to ice. She will spend her days in ice, trying to translate the stories her father told her into shadows cast from cold. She will translate her father's tales, and then she'll let them melt.

But before this, the girl will find herself in the restroom of the Wrist Institute surrounded by female Wrist Scholars who are washing their hands and fixing their hair and tucking white shirts into uniform skirts. She will find herself standing in the restroom looking in the mirror set low for her and she will be using her tongue to manipulate her now five loose teeth, when suddenly a horror she could only ever have imagined will unfold. She will watch her tongue push too hard and one of her teeth will fall into the valley between her gum and her lip. She will pull the tooth from its place and look at the jagged end, a part of her mouth now sitting in the palm of her hand. She will finger the place where the tooth left and then, with her tongue, she'll explore the void.

And so, before she becomes an ice sculptor and before she proves to her father that the wrist exists, she will come to the realization that she is not whole; that parts of her body fall out and off and will not reattach. She will learn that she is not a single being, but a network of linked catastrophes waiting to transpire.

In a revised introduction to the third edition of his *Wrist Discourse: Toward a Union of Hand and Arm*, her father the Wrist Scholar writes:

> My critics have called this book a personal attempt to understand my daughter's death, portrayed this volume not as a work of theory nor a case study, nor even a tale, but rather a confession. In light of such accusations, I have returned the book to the third person point of view, in an attempt to calcify the events precipitating her end such that I do not forget that children are not objects of study but manuscript drafts to be revised with great care.

In one of her last exhibits, the final line of the Ice Scupltor's *ars glacerium* reads:

> Imagine a room full of daughters. How is it different than a room full of girls?

THE GIRL WAITS IN her bed the tenth night of her fifth year, uses the bright light against the white wall as a stage for her shadows. She is thinking of her father's claim that a daughter is held inside a mother and trying to determine what this means. Does the daughter stand upright and grow along with the mother until the mother layer is shed to reveal the daughter underneath? Does the daughter split the mother like a flesh shell, then leave the mother behind, an abandoned suit? Perhaps every daughter was once a mother, but shed that past life. When she tries to make a shadow within another shadow, as the daughter is held inside the mother, she cannot make the logic work—she is left with only flat black on the pebbled tan of the Institute walls. But the question that loiters at the back of her mind, in the place where her hair meets her neck, is this: What is the role of the father in all this?

She is tracing the wall with her finger, outlining where she wants the shadow to live, when he knocks. It is 1 a.m. She slips back into bed and the door opens. His tie is loose and the buttons of his vest are undone such that the girl can see the suspenders that usually hide beneath his overcoat. He sits down on her bed and leans into her face, where his daughter meets him for a nose rub.

Good morning, he says. *Good morning, my love. Good morning, good morning, my child.* He looks at her for an unusually long time before she breaks his stare. *It has been a long day. For you, too?*

She nods her head. He has asked her this before, and she always agrees, though then she never meant it. *Strange how the day can seem longer when in fact it contains always the same number of hours.* He looks at her meager shelf of books, all of which concern her work with shadows: *Playing with the Dark, On Shadow Puppetry, Light and Image, The Art of the Shadow, Drawing on the Wall: A Sanctioning.* All the books contain photos of shaped shadow and light to mimic a variety of objects, a phenomenon she has been fascinated with since before she could speak.

In her *Attics and Wing Theory: Understanding Descent,* the woman the girl never called mother writes:

From a Room Studies perspective, the Allegory of the Womb allows us to see the relationship between the parlor and the foyer. That the former is an introduction to a larger structure and the latter is merely a walkway suggests that the notion of home is harbored not in centers, but in the arteries that act as channels from room to room. We have also to consider the role of attics, as the narrative's obsession with flight contributes to a rethinking of high rooms and their function within the larger structure. Stairs, then, become the method by which one ascends or descends, but not always—the implied reading swells beneath the surface, where stairs are not the only method of down. This dark truth is supported by statistics on both fatal attic falls and corpses found in upstairs rooms—these bodies are typically found either in beds or tubs, the two edifices that most easily invite relaxation during horizontal positioning.

The irony, of course, is that while most contemporary houses contain a room for living, we are careful to avoid acknowledging that some rooms are for death.

The girl's father does not think of his wife's words as he proceeds. *I do this for you, my love.* And the girl nods, though she does not understand what he does. *It is the right of everyone to know that the wrist is a myth. I do this so that you might live in a world where the truth is revealed and the word* wrist *is never uttered. This is a world I work to make real for you.*

The girl nods again, keeping her lips closed so as not to reveal the dark secret in her mouth: that her teeth—like the girls in his story—have left their place of origin. She has collected them in a jar that lives under her bed, the safest place she knows. She knows this because the one time she asked her father where her mother was, he said below, in the shade of underneath, and so she knows that anything that possesses the quality of under, such as her bed, or the dining hall tables, the trees with low-hanging branches in the Institute quad, is something to respect. In the jar are two of her teeth. Her jaw contains two empty plots and, she fears, more are to come, for four others are unstable. At the cafeteria, she chooses only liquids or pastes. She cannot risk hard food, for it may exacerbate the grave event unfolding in her mouth.

She knows crying cannot help and so resists, but when she wakes in the morning, her pillow is wet. She is starting to think that the force behind this cataclysm might not be language, and this thought she fears the most, for if speech is not the source, she cannot begin to imagine what might be.

But enough about work, the Wrist Scholar says, breaking his daughter's thought. *Rather, let's get back to the story. Tonight we'll share the narrative of The Barber and his Alice.*

Years later, when the Ice Sculptor is interviewed by an important art journal, she will be quoted as saying:

He thought that by stripping the world of a word, it would be saved. But he hadn't considered that language lives, and when it dies, it haunts. When he said *classify*, I heard *calcify*. This is why I have not changed.

THE BARBER AND HIS ALICE

A DAUGHTER SEEMS A simple thing. She bears purpose and potential, like a key or a road.

The Barber's Alice was drawn to fairy tales, and his favorite to retell dealt with that mysterious waving mass that burgeons from the skull. Women stuck in towers where hair became the rope that led them to their forest deaths; men who gained all power from their locks, who failed to protect these tresses from cunning women.

His daughter wore braids, thick braids that fell down her back and collected in the trench where her spine depressed. She spent her time outside in the fields, collecting—feathers and bones, weeds and rocks. Once she happened upon a pile of shells, the source of a story, since they made their home hundreds of miles from any body of water. She left the field early that evening, spent a full afternoon cleaning them gently with a soft brush. When her father returned, she had organized them in neat rows on her bed and was taking careful notes on each. He stood in the door for a while, watching her place a pencil behind her ear and finger the bumpy skin. Her braids met tidily at the center of her back. Later his wife would tell him their daughter called it *inventory*, the same way he noted and archived the state of his razor blades.

Because she spent all her time in the fields, her mother insisted they crop her hair in a short bob to help manage the matted mess. But the girl objected. So every night after her bath, her father would braid her curls and bind them with small metal clips.

At the barbershop, he carefully lathered necks, raked the minor rug of fur that coated men's cheeks and throats. His clients spoke of hard things: numbers, liquor, private wars. When he was done he would spin them slowly around to face the mirror. They would turn their heads slightly to one side, then the next, inspecting the work, while his gaze slid to the perimeter of the looking glass, where a photo of his daughter was snugly tucked.

The morning she went missing, while she was ushered to a dark elsewhere, his shears slipped and he accidently cut a man's neck. For an instant, he thought he'd not broken the skin, but then the blood surfaced along the oblong stretch that curved at the top and swung dramatically toward the place where the man's neck bent. He watched the event absently, failing to apologize until the man raised his palm to the nape and brought his hand to his face to witness the mess of hair-grit and blood.

On her bed lay her severed braids. The only thing missing other than her was the canning jar of shells. She was a smart girl, read her fairy tales as cautionary, not mere entertainment. After his shifts, he would roll five cigarettes and light them one after another, walk the ugliest streets of town, head down, hope raised, searching for her dropped shells.

He keeps the braids in his apron at work. This is how he traverses his days, grounded by the two healthy cords of woven hair that live in the deepest cove of his apron.

He removed the photo of his daughter from the corner of his mirror—too many folks knew and looked at it forlornly or didn't know and asked about her. The photo is retired to the same drawer where he keeps the blades. In his pockets live the braids, and throughout the day he dips his hands in and thumbs the bristles at the cropped end, daring to admire the careful, even cut.

FOR THE LATTER PART of the first month of her fifth year, the girl does not speak. She will not speak again until her sixth birthday, but she does not know this yet. The fear that her secret will be revealed permeates her every move, and she looks under the stalls in the Institute restroom before she parks herself in front of her tiny, low mirror to inspect the places where the teeth used to be.

It is a curse, she decides, but surely one she deserves. She has done something ghastly, irreparable, though she is unsure what. And so she stops speaking, both so no one notices the gaping absence in her mouth and so she saves herself from saying something that might inaugurate more loss—her ears or her fingers, her hair or her nails.

But a being, particularly one who has crested the precipice of age five, cannot successfully manage the lot of life alone. Too much loneliness, particularly at that age, can mean a condition settling in. And so the girl crafts the presence of others in her mind. First they are just abstract thoughts: three of them, like an ellipsis—uniform and united, pointing onward to denote a something else. But as her fifth year progresses and more of her teeth abandon her, the abstractions take shape on her wall and soon start to look distinctive: one a form that echoes a crushed hope; another an ill-formed idea; the final a memory, abandoned. In this way, the shapes she crafts become her cohort, and she releases the guilt and longing locked tight in her chest to her trifold shadow forms.

Meanwhile, her father continues his telling. And in the telling, the girl becomes further acquainted with the darkest logic of the world: that if something is begun—a meal or a journey, a story or a girl—it must always end.

Years later, after the girl who becomes an Ice Sculptor has left and is gone herself, the Multiversity of the Mid-North will name a room after her, and eventually a writer will want to tell her whole story because it strikes her as gothic. The Writer will sift through the Ice Sculptor's bookshelves and notes—the print catalog of the girl's life. The Writer will get a travel grant to conduct research on the Ice Sculptor's papers. On her visits to the Multiversity of the Mid-North, The Writer will end each evening with a shot of whiskey at a local bar because, while she knows that childhood is, essentially, a complicated system of ongoing discovered disappointments, she also knows that few lives can point to a single moment and deem it The Beginning of Childhood's End. The Writer will sip the whiskey tentatively from the miniscule glass and she will think that all the Ice Sculptor's sorrow gestures back toward the telling of a tale. The Writer will think briefly that her work as a writer is less about sharing a story and more about parsing together the loose strands of an unraveling fabric through which the character of the Ice Sculptor is threaded. The Writer will think she is less a writer and more an archivist. Then she will finish her shot.

THE BUTCHER AND HIS DOROTHY

THE BUTCHER WOULD COME home late, apron stained red and pink. His daughter would welcome him at the door. She would study the spatters while he carefully untied his boots in the mudroom. She would help him disrobe, and he taught her to safely roll the apron for storage before the next day's wash. They would then head to the sink and wash their hands together, she in front of him, standing on the stepstool he built for her, and he behind, his massive frame hovering over her so that he could smell the sweet and sweaty girlness in her hair. The Butcher would wrap his arms around her bony figure and they would share the water, passing the cake of soap back and forth, scrubbing their four palms and wrists, their nineteen fingers together in a tangle of nail and knuckle to confirm their cleanliness. Then they would dry their hands on fresh towels and he would carry her to bed.

He had lost his left ring finger in a botched chop during his first year at the slaughterhouse. This was before his daughter's birth, which meant she never knew that finger, understood it only as a gaping void in the grandeur of his hairy, calloused hand. She would ask him where the finger now lived and he would offer a series of conflicting stories: in a vast field of ice up north; riding waves in the warm ocean currents in the west; in a zeppelin ever-hovering over islands no one knew were there; in the eye of a storm that twisted and coiled far above them but never touched the earth.

After her death, he was ashamed to say he found great solace in the dark layers of meat at the slaughterhouse. The way that inside there exists a standardized order, one that follows the laws of wind-blown grain or cream in coffee, those swirling rows of tendon, the delicate layers of muscle curling and curving, the way music might look if we could see it. In a world where everything changed, he was comforted to know, when he broke open the body of a steer, the patterns of the beast persisted unadulterated. The night they found her, she was carried away before he could see the pile of gore that was his girl. Still, he lets himself think that had the someone who took her broke his daughter open the way he splits a steer, she would follow these same patterns, where an invisible code offers guide for the meat of all beasts. He is comforted to know that when he admires those muscles' delicate waves, he is not so far from her.

WHEN SHE IS NO longer a girl but an Ice Sculptor, she will do everything she can to resist remembering her fifth year, until one day it surfaces during a work session that proves fundamental to the development of her Cold Art Methodology. She will be wrapped in a sweatshirt that boasts Multiversity of the Mid-North, nose running and hands red-raw, working the ice with her file, and she will file harder because the ice is her past and then she will let the angle dip too much and she'll hear the crack in the center. She'll stand back and hear it growing, then use the sleeve of her sweatshirt to wipe away the dust of shaved ice. She will watch the crack slither south, jutting in several directions and sometimes resting, only to resume its arduous path. And as she watches the work become ruined by her hard hand, she will think of her father, how he was always so cold, how his hands would be cold, his feet, how he was always layered. What warms a father up? she will wonder, and watch her breath escape her mouth in clouds.

In an interview with *The Frozen Frieze* after she wins the prestigious Glacier Award for ice work, she will be asked about her methodology. In response, she'll say she carves the ice with steam, which allows manipulation without rupturing the work. It is a skill she'll say she learned from her father.

THE MILLER AND HIS DOROTHY

THE MILLER'S DAUGHTER WAS a girl of promise. She often wandered through the streets all day to conjure playful tales. At night, she would relay them to her father and he would listen, in awe of her gift for telling, always wondering from where, in the forms of her mother and himself, the source of the gift derived. The Miller's daughter told him these tales from her bed as he sat on a chair in the corner in the dark, a position he took because she insisted. When he had been closer, where she could see his face, it somehow influenced her telling, changing the trajectory of the tales as they escaped her. And so the father sat alone in the corner, his face kept hidden from his daughter, whose narratives filled the room.

One night, she told him the beginning of a tale so haunting that it shook him to the core. And just as he was finding himself unable to stop his body from shaking, right there in the middle, his daughter told him that she would be concluding the narrative for the night, leaving her audience hovering above the end. The father asked—in a voice that lingered on the edge of pleading—if she would finish the tale, please finish the tale tonight, for he could not survive the suspense for even one day. The daughter giggled, then said she was sorry, that she could not tell him the end because of a very simple fact: she did not yet know it. When The Miller asked in a whisper if she could invent it, please, my darling, just this once and for tonight, the daughter smiled. Dear father, she told him, do you not know the first rule of story? Endings are not invented; they are discovered.

He praised her tale and bid her good evening, though he could not bring himself to kiss her forehead as he always did. And when he took himself to bed, lying next to the woman his daughter called mother, he struggled to find sleep. Through the night, he was left in the twilight space on the border of waking, the tale a vortex in which he found himself consumed. His fear was two-fold: both that the story's conclusion might be more horrific than the tale so far, and that the story's origin lived somewhere inside the body he'd co-produced.

The next day at the mill, weary-eyed, groggy, and expended by the tale, The Miller struggled to work. He found himself making minor mistakes. As he left the mill for fresh air, he forgot to firmly fasten the door. Meanwhile, his daughter had spent the morning wandering the streets in order to find the story's ending, and just as The Miller left, she entered the site of his work, so excited to share with him the conclusion that she could not keep her body still. Her exhilaration made her form unfamiliar to her—she tried to control it but she continued to fail, tripping on the stone path from the town's center, losing her footing again as she half ran to the mill. And so, when she reached it, she accidentally fell into the complex machination that—until that moment—had practiced annihilation only in an effort to produce.

In the years to come, The Miller would tell no one the story of his lost girl. For what haunts The Miller is why he's haunted: not because his daughter's gone, but because he has been left for eternity ever-hovering in the horror of the story she left undone.

By the time the girl has acclimated to the age of five but before she is on her way toward six, she will be woken one morning to a discovery concerning her mouth that will confuse her even further. She will wake in her small room with the light still on, because she had fallen asleep while working with her shadow girls. As the light of the morning filters into the room from the tiny window that lives high up on the wall, it melts with the artificial light of her lamp, in effect putting her shadow friends to sleep. She wakes and notes this, then runs the tip of her tongue along the bottom gums, where two coves sit empty. But as she lets her tongue linger in the fissure left behind, she notes a bit of rigid something emerging from where her tooth no longer lives.

The walk to the women's restroom feels much longer than usual. As she takes each cautious step, she tries not to visualize what could be growing in the caverns of her mouth. She imagines a claw emerging that curves toward her eyes and envelopes her face. She imagines a mechanism planted in her gums by someone she trusts while she is sleeping, one that slowly grows over and around the contours of her head to lock it closed like a fitted cage. But when she places herself in front of her low mirror and, after sighing deeply, opens her mouth, what she sees is a slice of bone-white. She runs her tongue along it and then places her tiny index finger in the hole to confirm.

It is more ragged at the top than the last, but it feels like—could it be?—another tooth. She is so relieved that she slides to the ground. She almost wants to smile until a foggy sadness overwhelms her, as she comes to realize that her comfort might be short-lived, that just because a new one's coming in does not mean it will stay. Perhaps her crime is so fundamentally awful she has been sentenced to a lifetime of rotating teeth, where her mouth is a machine that churns out bone like the head makes hair.

She walks back to her room alone, and when she passes her father in the hall, she does not return his nod.

AFTER THE ICE SCULPTOR's passing, a series of ice sculpture publications will contact the Wrist Scholar in an effort to interview him about his daughter's death. He will have the staff of the Wrist Institute hold off these calls and visits, but one will sneak through. The Writer will craft a fiction that she is a cousin of the Wrist Scholar and wants to pay her respects. When the staff grants her entrance, she will be directed to the Ice Sculptor's girlhood bedroom first. She will slowly turn the doorknob and she will enter the room.

THE WOODSMAN AND HIS DOROTHY

CONTROL, THAT DARK DESIRE, rules the heart of the father and the daughter, for it is the evolved apparatus for combating fear. Of all the species gracing the ground, the quality of character fathers and daughters share most closely is the paralyzing anxiety installed by threatened governance.

For years he practiced the art of control, spent hours in his room entertaining his daughter who did not speak. The source of her silence was a dark mystery that cloaked the home like an opaque blanket covers a sick child. The Woodsman tried in vain to draw a smile from his daughter's lips and one day did when he whittled a face into a log. By the time he had manufactured a full marionette, the girl smiled daily, watching him work the image of the child out of the wood, watching the wood child released from the confines of the logs. When finally the child was done, body-clothed, face-painted, and string-secure, the girl's desire to be heard overwhelmed her. Her father handed her the puppet and she began to use its body as a language, to speak through the wooden frame and to her father. In this way, he learned her fears and needs. She loved best watching her father manipulate the strings such that the wooden child looked as though it moved alone. She would watch her father's show, let herself be seduced by the movement of the wooden child, but soon she let her gaze slide up to the scaffolding: her father's hands moving the beast's acts below. His hands worked not unlike a maker of music—fingers dipping, wrists angled and sweeping through the air, her father looking south with eyebrows raised and head tilted. And because fathers get lonely, too, the Woodsman spent time with the wooden child even when his real child wasn't watching. The Woodsman spent his days learning to move the body with increasing accuracy and agility until watching the wooden child meant also forgetting that there was a meat-and-skin man orchestrating the act. Eventually, he was ashamed to admit there was nothing that could have replaced the wooden being he moved, that the power exercised by the dance of his hands was an art and a science at once, a magic and a math.

He had always been careful to put the puppet away, for he knew the risk of rope; he had lost his father to it. And although that had required intention, he knew that a similar end could be met by mistake. But four years to the day after his wife had succumbed to her sickness, he drank too much of the liquor he'd been keeping in the cellar in the barrel branded with her name.

He shudders to think of the mess he left on the floor; the pile of chord and limb, two faces—one wood and one flesh—cheek to cheek. He shudders because for a fraction of a second he admires the way they are entwined, the way he cannot tell where his offspring ends and his art begins.

He is still concerned with puppetry, but is unable to touch his wooden forms and their adjacent string. Now it is more a matter of silent shape, less with voice and walk. He only performs shows for himself, and does decorative woodwork for the townsfolk: simple and elegant adornments like floral designs to frame their cutting boards, decorative pulls for dresser drawers.

He imagines his failure as a father is his best trait as an artist, for as hard as he looked, he could not find the invisible strings directing his little girl. He wonders what artist manages her strings now.

WHEN SHE IS EIGHT, in line to get dinner in the cafeteria, the girl will ask her father why he does not believe in the wrist. Several of the Wrist Scholar's students will be in line behind her and overhear this question. They will stop and look up at the scholar in preparation for his answer. He will ladle soup into his bowl and look at his daughter, then at his students. He will tell her he does not have time to explore the intricacies of the field; that if she is truly interested, she can read the introduction to his first book.

Later that evening, the girl will slip out of her tiny room to wash her face before bed in the Institute's women's restroom. When she returns, a book will lie on her pillow, with a red ribbon marking a place. She will open *Against the Wrist* and read the following:

Wrist Studies, while trying to chronicle the controversial history of the place where the hand and arm meet, attempts to understand why our culture has grown dependent on the myth of the wrist. Contemporary scholars believe the notion of the wrist matriculated out of early theories of the wing. There is suspicion that the myth of the wrist is rooted in the human desire to fly and the psychological implications of learning we cannot, a devastating discovery that permeates our existence and encourages resentment toward the concept of gravity. In effect, Wrist Studies considers one of its primary goals discovering where in our psyches is rooted this innate need. Wrist Studies also has a particular investment in the preservation and scholarly investigation of underground wrist gardens and their keepers.

But above all, the field of Wrist Studies concerns itself with this central question: where does the hand end and the arm begin?

THE SMITH AND HIS ALICE

A MAN CARES FOR his wife for a very long time. Then she becomes withchild and he cares for her even more, knowing the empty channel inside of her is full of the rest of his story, the next link in the family chain. In this way, his wife becomes a room in which is locked his minute future.

He lost his wife in childbirth. She, the room in which the child developed, then left empty and gone. She, a room buried, such that another house might be built atop.

This is how the girl that came from her was his and his alone. And because the girl was then his everything, he managed her with great care, learned when to lock her doors and when to keep them open, learned how to break the hinge to get inside.

Now a man with white hair and sagging skin, he has trouble remembering exactly how that day unfolded, though it still ambles through his mind at odd times. He had locked her in, slid the key under the door. *No one*, he had told her, and she had said back, *No one*, and these were the last words he heard leave her lips. Some way down the path he had looked back, saw the dark outline of his girl peering out the window.

It is when he cannot find the key that he knows. The door sustained no damage, which meant only one thing: when she said *No one*, she had lied.

Sometimes he thinks of his girl—her portrait lingers in the fissures of his memory—but through the years she has grown in his mind. She is a woman with children of her own, big-hipped like her mother, strong chin and small hands and gruff voice.

And sometimes he thinks of where that key lives now, because he knows the properties of metal. Is it buried like his wife, earth working on the body like weather? Has it been melted in a furnace, rebuilt as a tiny metal doll? Or does it live on a string that dips between the breasts of his daughter, rusted around the edges from her sweat? He thinks these things when he mends a hinge and swings it to ensure it is quiet, when he rattles a knob to confirm security—he thinks these things when he sees the empty frame of a way without a door.

IN HER PENULTIMATE BOOK, *On Departing and Apartment*, the woman the girl never called mother writes:

> Bound to the idea that our arms are in fact perversions of real winghood, it stands that we are, for the most part, failed birds, flightless and grounded.

IF SHE COULD OPEN her mouth, she would like to ask:

Where do the Dorothies go?

What color is The Barber's daughter's hair? Why did her father not reveal this in the telling of his story?

When the fathers of lost daughters tell each other stories, is the way they sit more a circle or a horseshoe?

Do the Alices ever think of coming home?

Since the fathers of lost daughters gather on top floors, are they ever scared of heights?

What does her father like better: studying wrists or fathering her?

Is she a Dorothy or is she an Alice, and when will she find out?

If her father lost his daughter, would he go to meetings of the fathers of lost daughters, and if so, what would his story be?

WHEN THE GIRL IS eleven, she will attend one of her father's lectures without his knowledge. She will slink into the back of the lecture hall and keep her bangs low across her face so he can't make her out. She will bury her nose in a notebook like the others, but she will only pretend to write. Instead, the girl will watch her father, notice how he carries himself differently during oration, keeps his hands behind his back, tilts his chin up a bit. She will think he looks much smaller from this height, though his voice booms throughout the lecture hall. Smaller not just in size but in scope; he is somehow reduced from this angle. Volume, she will think, must be applicable not just to sound and mass but to form.

He will say:

Believers in the wrist suggest that proof exists in theories of the neck—the union of the head to the chest and shoulder space. They purport the same logic provides a framework for validating the existence of the wrist, though bone scholars have disagreed, as the primary difference between the two is that the neck contains vital organs. Furthermore, there is a wide body of literature on the history of hangings and the valuable role the neck plays in this discourse. Relationships have been drawn between the wrist and ankle, but these, too, are false, given the heel's value in literature of the joint. Correlations between the wrist and knee or elbow are seldom drawn, given that these act as space breaks in the leg and arm; both do not adhere two separately identified parts, but rather act as an interruption in the rhetoric of limb.

We say that tables have legs and chairs have arms. We say that books have spines and bottles have necks. We say that clocks have hands; we say that shoes have tongues. The notion of the wrist, however, has not been admitted into the domain of dead metaphor—in short, nothing else contains a wrist.

In short, we will lose nothing if we choose to lose the wrist.

THE ANGLER AND THE WAINWRIGHT AND THEIR ALICE

BECAUSE LOVE IS A complex system of overlapping greetings and departures, the places where love ends and begins is often obscured. While popular belief maintains that the body is the conduit for love, it is in the mind where love buds and breaks open and apart. And because the mind is a mysterious arena that is enveloped in comings and goings that intersect and knot like a dense web, it induces a variety of dread. This is why there are no Scholars of Love.

The Angler had met a woman for whom he cared. When she said she wanted a child, he felt giving her one would be a very kind gift. He would leave for weeks out to sea to lead his girls toward a proper life. Soon after the child arrived, he left for too many moons, and on his return he was not welcomed at the door because the woman had become mind-sick and then became gone. This is how the woman thanked him for his gift: she gave it back.

The Angler could not pursue his fishing ventures with the tiny girl at home, so he went to the village to see about more grounded work. On the way through the center of the village, his daughter holding his hand, The Angler spotted The Wainwright working on a wagon in distress. As they came closer, his daughter squeezed her father's hand, because tucked into the place where his shirt met his neck was a flower of a very rare shade. It was a shade living on the precipice between the colors that she knew. It was a shade that collapsed those more familiar colors, that was even somehow missing from the magic in the sky that bloomed in the aftermath of storm.

And when the daughter and The Angler approached The Wainwright, he knew without looking up what they were there for and untethered the flower from his neck, handed it to the girl. Then he looked at The Angler with a smile that was also an invitation.

The Wainwright came to The Angler's home that evening and The Angler told him all: about the woman and the gift and the disgrace he experienced at the peace of her release. And how wrong she always felt. And his shame at feeling most at home in the middle of the sea. And with the thin bone carcasses of emptied fish still left on the table, The Wainwright kissed The Angler's forehead and then moved slowly toward The Angler's lips. Then he took The Angler's hand and led him to the bed.

Their Alice would watch The Wainwright mend wagons, and for every day The Angler was on a ship and the duo at home would be overcome with sadness at his being gone, they would make a notch in the door, so that when The Angler returned he could see how much they missed him. And The Wainwright would take the girl on long trips in the carts he fixed and she would see what lingered far beyond the village. And when The Wainwright would tuck her in at night, the girl would tell him that when she became old she would spend all her days searching for the mystical color that marked The Wainwright that very first day.

It was a year after the girl had begun to call The Wainwright Other Father and it was during a storm. The Angler returned to shore because he could read the sky and knew far worse was coming. When his home was in view, he saw The Wainwright approaching through heavy sheets of rain. From far away, their embrace looked gentle, but up close the truth was revealed: The Wainwright was keeping The Angler from falling to his knees.

It stormed for three days and they spent the whole time searching the wood, asking around the village, retracing every parcel of land they had ever let the girl traverse. They did not eat or sleep. They spent the storm apart.

They were cradling each other in bed when The Angler looked out the window to see the mystical shade that had marked The Wainwright that first day was smeared across the sky. He shuddered then and rose to close the curtain.

WHEN SHE IS TWELVE, she will ask her father how he entered the field of Wrist Studies. He will take off his glasses and place his thumb and middle finger on his nose. He will breathe in deeply and look her in the eye, then put his glasses back on. He will pull from his shelf a first edition of *Wrist Discourse: Toward a Unity of Arm and Hand*, flip to the opening pages, and hand her the book. When she starts to read it, he will ask if she could take it to her room, as he is very busy. She will go there and read these words:

> The leading scholar in the field of Wrist Studies cites a single moment in his discovery of the field. When clasping a bracelet on his daughter, he was taken by the fact that it seemed to fall either on her hand or her arm. When he asked his daughter to point to her wrist, the daughter pointed to her head. Wrists, he then concluded, are a social construction perpetrated by our need to categorize the body. Subsequently, his life's work became stripping the world of the wrist.

THE ICE SCULPTOR'S MOST successful work will be a series of exhibits in which she hangs hands formed of ice from lines bound to the ceiling. A series of studio lights will be adhered to the ground on the opposite side of the room, and when the lights are administered, the wall will reveal a set of shadow puppets in all shapes. Fruit and books and ladders. Mugs and bathtubs. Aged spoons and empty closets. Agony and flight.

The shadows are sustained on the wall for a brief period of time, until the light that allows the shadow to form induces melt. The exhibit is titled *Suspension of Belief.*

IN THE FIRST VOLUME she published after meeting the Wrist Scholar—the book titled *Rooms and Crime*—the woman the girl never called mother writes:

> The human voice rises when questions are asked, therein adhering the notion of up with the unknown. This logic—unknown is up, known is down—is further perpetrated by the use of upper and lower case in parsing out the difference between specific and general ideas. That the upper case contains the letters we use to denote the grand theories of life such as Death, Fear, and Love further yokes the notion of up with that which is unknown, for the general and abstract—the intangible and fluid—is capitalized not because these terms harbor more significance, but because they will endure as concepts forever defined and redefined, a salve we apply to the wound of mystery.
>
> It is in this way that our notion of unknown is bound to and rooted in up. And it is in this way that the harvesting of knowledge implicitly requires the agent to go down.

THE GIRL IS IN her room working with her three shadow girls, when her father enters at 1 a.m.

Hello, child, he says, adjusting his tie. *Are you well?*

She wants to say No. She wants to say No, I am not, I am very unwell because, you see, my mouth has become an independent organism. But she keeps her lips closed. She nods to him. And then he nods to her.

As you are entering this last quarter of your fifth year, it is time to introduce a conflict to the plot, her father says. *Tonight we'll hear The Mystery of the Archivist's Daughter.*

When she is ten, she will participate in her first ice-sculpting exhibition. It will be held at the local cold space, where Ice Sculptors from across the country have come to evaluate amateur work. She will wait for her father all evening, and even as she is receiving the praise of the professionals and getting her ribbon for first place, her father will not be there. Just as the local cold space guardians are telling her to leave, her father will arrive. She will grab his hand in hers and lead him swiftly to the dome, and he will quicken his pace as they navigate the labyrinths of sculptures. But already she will be anticipating the worst. And when they arrive, the worst will be realized, as they meet only a dark blue ribbon in the center of a puddle.

THE MYSTERY OF THE ARCHIVIST'S DAUGHTER

THE RIDDLE IS THIS: The Archivist's daughter is neither a Dorothy nor an Alice. The fathers have theories, but the question remains. If not dead or missing, how lost could The Archivist's daughter be?

INDEED, HOW LOST COULD The Archivist's daughter be?, the girl will think as she tries to sleep that evening. She had thought her father's tales were merely to warn her, but now her curiosity is piqued. This is a riddle, she concludes, and riddles are solved only one way.

The stories of the Lost Daughter Collective have haunted her since the first time her father introduced her to The Realm of the Real the night before—Or was it the morning of? When in the twilight time between sleep and waking does the day begin?—she turned five. The nights he comes to tell her of the Lost Daughter Collective, she is haunted by the tales of the fathers, but on the nights when he does not come, she imagines what kind of stories the daughters would tell.

And this is how her shadow girls become lost daughters, each of whom has her own side of the story. And while she knows it is dangerous territory to imagine, she cannot help thinking that while the fathers see their girls as lost, perhaps the girls interpret their leaving differently.

She has been working on a piece she calls *Exit Father*, wherein her three shadow girls perform their tales to an audience of fathers in order to teach them how to better take on their role. Just as her father lectures to his students, there is a message to be found in her piece, if he chooses to listen.

It is the conclusion of *Exit Father*, the closing moments after the girls have shared their tales, that impresses her most. As a final gesture, the three forms come ever closer until they finally connect, unite, grow into and around each other. And then, in a breathtaking climax, she empties the form, so that it stands not as a compendium of shadow, but as the compendium's frame.

This is how she takes the daughters that are lost and makes them found.

IN HER FINAL PUBLISHED book, *The Room with Two Doors*, the woman the girl never called mother writes:

> Which is the entrance? Which is the exit? How is it decided which role each serves? And who decides in which direction the current runs? The room with two doors has always a line of people walking through it. This is the case through light and dark hours, through ages of water and through ages of ice.
>
> The people who walk through the room with two doors do not know that they do so. One of the people is you.

Good morning, my only *child, and happy birthday*, her father says at 1 a.m. She has been six for one hour. He stands next to her where she is tucked into the bed, her two hands holding the even cuff of the bed sheets.

I am in the final edits of the new book, so I cannot stay long, but I did want to congratulate you on adding yet another year to your repertoire. The Wrist Scholar looks at his daughter, who looks up at him with large eyes.

Your face, he tells her. *Your face is growing lean. Your face is becoming the face of a woman*, he tells her, and she blinks twice.

As you are now six, you will notice other things changing, too, he tells her. *As the body moves through the years, it grows and sheds accordingly. Do not be surprised if you begin to lose things or discover development in places you might not have anticipated.*

The girl does not feel her face flush or realize she's opened her mouth. It does not register that she needs to visit the restroom. With the delivery of her father's words is erased the knowledge that she is in fact corporeal. And when her tiny jaw falls and her lips part, her father squints to see inside her mouth.

Well, but you've already started! The teeth are the first to go. But now I must be telling you things you've known for months. It is true what they say: as the daughter develops, she needs the father less. The Wrist Scholar pats the girl on the head twice. *Good morning, and happy birthday, my only,* he says and walks out the door.

The girl does not notice that he does not lean in for the touching of her nose to his. The girl does not notice that there is no narrative tonight. The girl notices nothing, because her cognition is obfuscated by the process of knowledge slowly budding in the mind.

The girl sits letting this knowledge overtake her for some time before the desire to visit the restroom prompts her to leave. And as she lowers her pajama bottoms and climbs the toilet to seek the comfort of release, she finds that she cannot. She cannot void herself, and she cannot cry. She wants to cry for her fifth year and her mother and for the curse of misunderstanding and for keeping quiet and for not knowing the rules of daughterhood.

Eventually she gives up. The girl exits the restroom and walks quietly to the dining hall. When she enters, it is empty, chairs living sideways on the table, floor shining, the smell of clean. In the door that leads from the dining hall to the parking lot, she notices the silhouette of a figure smoking. When she gets closer, the woman turns around and the girl sees it is she who dishes up food three times a day.

What are you doing awake? the woman says, waving the smoke from her eyes.

I would like a cup of water, the girl says.

We're out of water, the woman tells her. *But I can get you something else.*

Here— the woman says, handing her a tall cup full of ice. *This ice is enchanted. Put the glass aside and go to sleep. When you wake tomorrow, you'll have a glass of water,* the woman says.

The girl holds the cup of ice with two hands. She peers into the well of the cup. The woman watches her for a minute while she fixes her hairnet and corrects her apron, shoves her fist into her thick hip. She takes a drag, then squints and leans her head toward the girl. *Are you okay?*

The girl nods.

As soon as the woman turns around, the girl decides she does not believe in enchantment. And so she does not set the cup aside. Instead she studies the ice, watches it contract and condense, watches it crack and shift and fall. And when at last there is only a nub of ice left floating at the top of what is now a glass of water, she decides she is done with shadow and will only deal in melt.

That night she says goodbye to her shadow girls. They beg her not to end them, but she tells them there is no such thing in history as going back.

By morning, she has buried her three shadow girls in light and decided that six will be a better year.

IN HER POSTHUMOUSLY PUBLISHED book *Access to the Exit: The Imperceptible Door*, the woman the girl never called mother writes:

> The Allegory of the Womb purports a body is only distinct from its surroundings if we cast that body as part of the foreground, not the back. Consider this:

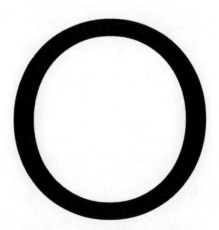

> You may think this is a sphere, but you are looking inside, not out:

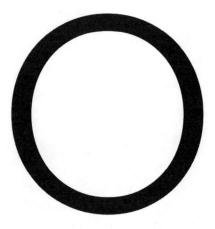

Now you see it is not a sphere, but rather a hole in a wall.

Just as we think we can tell the foreground from the back, the inside from the out, the mother from the daughter, we think that we tell our stories. But I am here to tell you: our stories tell us.

HER FINAL EXHIBIT WILL be titled *Against Rational Daughterhood.* In it, the exhibit floor becomes a mouth and she lines it with giant teeth. But unlike her other projects, this one resists melt. After the teeth maintain their shape for an eerie length of time, and after the viewer is compelled to move closer to the work, the secret is revealed. The teeth are not crafted from ice, but glass.

IN HER LAST INTERVIEW, when The Writer asks her a question about her father, she will say she does not want to talk about him. When The Writer insists, the Ice Sculptor will respond aggressively and then regret it and ask The Writer not to publish what she said. The Writer will leave the comment out of the publication, but after the Ice Sculptor's death, The Writer will resurrect her words. Paired with the radical departure from ice featured in her final exhibit, the statement will become the anachronistic last words of the Ice Sculptor. Her proclamation that day and the phrase that resonates in every mind who will come to hear the Ice Sculptor's story is this:

> My father's theories suggest possibility is not a branching forth, the opening of a web. My father's theories suggest possibility is a many-tiered grave in which all of the not is buried.
>
> When I was young, he took away my arms, but I did not lose my hands; they stay hovering next to where my wrists should be.

PART II:

THE REGION OF PERHAPS

Neverland is more or less an island.

—*Peter*

COME NIGHTS, THE GIRLS would ask, each alone in their separate homes across the contours of the country and the zones that designate time: *Tell the story of the ice girl and her father without whisks.*

Risks, their fathers would say, making dinner or folding laundry, doing the dishes or picking up their dolls. *Her father without risks,* they'd say, and launch the telling of the tale. *Once, long ago, there was a man who lived life without risks,* they would tell their daughters, and the girls would listen, looking up at their fathers with wide eyes.

This was when thought was very powerful and there were books. In fact, the ice girl and her father lived in a Language Museum, where people talked together about notions all day. The displays at the Language Museums were called prophecies and those who populated the museum exhibits were called prophessors. One prophessor cared deeply for his thinking. In fact, he enjoyed thinking with others so much that he seldom had time to think with his daughter, and because so many of our methods of growing up are rooted in learning from our parents, she was not told some very important things. And so she was horrified when events began to unfold for which she was unprepared. As a result, she did not speak for an entire year.

She grew up to carve ice using heat because it reminded her of the way her father treated her. And that, the fathers would say, towering over their daughters, *is why fathers and daughters should always be close and transparent.*

The daughters would nod several times and then ask Is dinner ready? or Can I help? or Tuck me in! and the fathers would respond reflexively Yes, No, Sure, with the story still loitering in the back of their heads.

This was the refrain the men would repeat for their girls before the daughters died or went missing.

This is the mantra they now repeat together at the meetings of the Fathers of Lost Daughters, or the FOLD:

> Every woman was once a girl,
> and every girl was once a daughter.
> For every woman in the world
> there will always be laughter in slaughter.

The Fathers of Lost Daughters gather on the top floor of an abandoned umbrella factory in the downtown of a small city. The group is composed of men who meet weekly to mourn. Along with the roomful of fathers, there is always strong coffee and a healthy supply of a tasteless biscuit. A rich store of kerchiefs is hidden in the pockets and palms of the men so as not to invite tears. Despite this, crying often ensues, though the men use their sleeves so as not to dirty the kerchiefs their girls wove for them.

The men gather regularly to share their narratives or to sit without speaking in a kind of vigil. The group was founded on the theory that when beings gather, grief moves among them, dispersing rather than multiplying, and in this way their mourning is communal.

Today is the hardest day of the year for the FOLD. They arrive at dawn and will not break their meeting until nightfall. This is done as defense against the devastation that lingers on the borders of the day: the compulsion to join their daughters' status as lost. They gather to secure their own safety. Today is the day that is called Daughter's Day.

The men think of all the things that will not happen to and with their girls: every wound left unkissed, every hand left unheld, every bath the fathers did not nor will ever draw. They travel from all corners of the city, and the paths they take form an obscure constellation that can only be interpreted by a child. The shape of their travel looks something like the thin fingers and palm of a human hand, and they enter the top floor of the umbrella factory at the place where the hand should meet the arm.

The FOLD consists of the following members: Nero Barber, Silas Butcher, Lars Woodsman, Salvador Smith, Tristram Angler, Octavio Wainwright, Ignatius Miller, and their leader, known only as Peter.

At night the fathers fall to sleep yearning for youth with tears. In this way, the Fathers of Lost Daughters revert to sons.

WHEN THE FATHERS RECALL the events that transpired, the stories yoke so that the girls are understood as a single assemblage. This is not a practice overtly instituted, but one that slowly transpired because they did not use their daughters' names. Eventually the network of daughter-exit was understood less as a long list of lost girls and more as an intricate design before which the men stood in awe. Their stories and their grief, once ambulant and varied, live now in a narrative that hovers and coils around the safe space of the thirty-third floor of the abandoned umbrella factory.

The ice girl, tell the story of the ice girl, the daughters would ask separately and now, through narrative, together.

Again? That's twice this week.

It is a story that never grows old, the girls would respond, and tug on their father's hands or shirtsleeves, back pockets or pant legs.

The ice girl had three maidens that accompanied her always through the form of shadows. They were called Mary, Charlotte, and Virginia. They, too, had fathers who stayed distant. They, too, were artists, but they did not work with ice—they were archivists. They collected the world's events in their heads and then filtered them through language until art remained. The consumption of this art was called reading.

Reeding? Like the wood part of an instrument?

In the sense that there is a kind of reverberation, yes. And in the sense that this all happened on paper, which was made of wood, yes.

What is paper?

A thin material like lace, only it could cut you. Eventually it was outlawed because it was too dangerous. It is the tool by which archivists used to make their art.

How do they make it now?

They don't. Archivists are extinct.

The girls would think on that, the idea of extinction, how it was a kind of end that grows ever greater. Their fathers had told them that extinction is like waiting in a very long line for a ticket that takes you to the back of the line, where you started.

The fathers would see the look on their daughters' faces. *But all this was before The Touch Wars,* the fathers would say, to ease the worry in their brows.

And then, in unison, the daughters—in their separate homes, in a variety of pastel-colored pajamas, holding a gamut of stuffed animals—would ask, *What were The Touch Wars?*

THE TOUCH WARS IS the anthropological label given to an era in collective memory in which it was believed that touch among humans was too prevalent and entering the realm of criminal. Such touch—between lovers, among colleagues, within families—was dissuaded through statewide campaigns that raised awareness about the dangers of touch in transmitting disease or relaying misinterpreted affection.

As a result of The Touch Wars, a period of two decades passed wherein a rapid decline in childbirth ensued, the obvious result of touch-lack. The reciprocal effects were surprisingly rich; people spent their time making art, and, released of their financial responsibility to secure the present and future of multiple others, were left to engage in more leisure. Couples, in an attempt to dissuade the desire for touch, spent much of their time seeing places they did not know existed. Such a time is believed to have been one of the happiest in this region's history.

But soon enough, people started to recognize the limits of such a life. Care for the land's older population was the first inclination that touch-lack might be problematic, as citizens' parents and elder generations were quickly ushered out of life without physical contact. Touch, corporeal archeologists began to understand, was both a curse, ushering in touch-crime, but also a vital tenant contributing to longer lives. Too, after years of keeping touch to themselves, people began to desire each other in ways that permeated their bodies and minds. Such drive was contained through self-touch for many years, but it was made clear that the integrity of partner union was founded less on the discoveries of corporeal archeologists and more in ancient literature, where themes such as understanding, adoration, and dread dissolved. The result was a radical movement that began in the major cities where citizens would, behind closed doors and in a variety of rooms, engage in all brands of touch. It is said that groups would gather and spend hours holding hands—in large circles, in small groups, in pairs that traded on and off. It was a time where trans-skin union was reinstated in the collective memory—through the act of hand-holding, people began to remember what it meant to feel heat radiate off another, and in the aftermath of this collective discovery, empathy blossomed.

The Museum of Paternal Understanding offers perhaps the only vestige of The Touch Wars. This complex era in history is preserved at this site, where even today can be heard the prescriptive "Please don't touch."

However, recent trends in touchology are encouraging engagement with exhibits. This revolution in experiential museum-going inaugurates an acceptance that touch is human, necessary, vital. But with the exit of the notion of not touching in museums, the complex history of The Touch Wars may lose its last link to contemporary life, and therefore dissolve into the growing void that is history lost.

And this is why we tell the history of The Touch Wars, because it reminds us of perhaps the most important lesson we can teach: we do not tell our stories to share; we tell our stories to warn.

THE FOLD AIMS ONLY to get through the day together, though a mystery looms over the group. Last week their leader, known only as Peter, told them that today will be his final meeting.

In the moment they were told, the men struggled to believe. Barber even stood up, ready to protest, but Butcher pulled him back down. The news that their leader was leaving surfaced in their minds throughout the week leading toward today. It felt like a personal, intimate rupture in the fabric of their group. A group like the FOLD relies on a delicate balance of folly and fear—they must serve as bereavement associates, chaperoning optimism while also staying vigilant that hope does not soil the mind. The manager of such sorrow serves as both a liaison and a guard, a role not easily filled. And this is how, without Peter, the system may collapse.

What do you make of Peter's claim? Butcher asks. It will be a particularly difficult Daughter's Day, the men think, because the day is breaking beautifully.

Barber blows his nose. *I am at a loss.*

I am taking it personally. I know that it's not, Smith says, looking up at the tall rafters that populate the ceiling, *but it feels that way.*

The men are interrupted by the sound of Wainwright and Angler entering the room. Peter always insisted on punctuality, but what circulates without being said is that Peter has still not arrived. Wainwright sits down and Angler heads to the table to pour himself a cup of coffee. *I'm sorry we're late*, Wainwright tells the group, and no one says anything back. He sits next to Woodsman and touches him on the shoulder, leaning in. *I could barely get him out of bed*, he whispers. *It's a miracle we're here.* When Miller clears his throat, they give him their attention.

Let's not be acute, Miller says, addressing the group. As he speaks, he looks out the window across the cityscape. *You can read it in his body. He is tired of being sad.* Miller turns around to look at the other men, his voice growing louder as he speaks. *And isn't that what we all hope for? A moment when we might feel again what it is like to wake and not think of her? Don't we all want to return to the men we were in the time before her loss, when we led more stable, simpler lives?*

Keep your voice down, Butcher says. *Can someone shut the door?*

Please—, Smith says too loudly, and all the men look up. *Please*, he says, *leave the door open.*

And because they all know the story of his daughter, they comply.

For me, right now, says Barber, returning to the issue at hand, *it is less about finding the shore and more about keeping afloat.*

But I do see what you mean, Angler says. *I don't want to be craving this group for the rest of my life. I want to be reaching a place where I can wake not needing our meetings. That is my goal.*

And that, I suspect, is how Peter feels now, Miller says. *He can't be blamed for overcoming.*

The men take a sip of coffee or run their hands through their hair. One picks at the dead skin on the tip of his thumb, while outside the bells chimes eight.

PETER HAS A THEORY that their daughters live in places the men cannot access—abstract and mysterious places, like those over a rainbow or down a rabbit hole. Peter calls these places the Lands of Never, the places that cannot be reached. This is because adults do not know how to traverse this terrain. It is knowledge firmly locked in a child.

But on their walks home, after the men disperse from their meetings, they cannot help but imagine that they, too, had the capacity to visit the Lands of Never when they were young, though they did not. They, too, possessed the intrinsic map of these lands, but chose to roam the Lands of Now.

And just before they reach their doorsteps, as they are about to enter their homes, they pose the question aloud, in the raw autumn, enmeshed in the smell of change; through a screen of mist in late spring; in the early dark of winter, the silence frail: where are her Lands of Never, and how can I get there?

The matrix of possibility that suggests where she might be plagues them, but there is a darker truth at work. For the men fail to realize that the Lands of Never are not about where but when.

How did the shadow *maidens help the ice girl if they could not speak?* their daughters would ask, before they entered their several Lands of Never, while still bound to the Lands of Now.

No, no, it was the ice girl who could not speak. The shadow maidens talked to her through their shadow forms, as this was when shadow was a language. The shadow maidens were daughters whose fathers thought they were, in different ways, failed. The fathers wanted very much for their daughters to fit certain archaic standards, but their daughters did not. And so the daughters left.

The girls would look up at their fathers then with large eyes, trying to imagine why any daughter would leave. Perhaps that is how fatherhood ends? The girls shook the thought from their heads.

What were books like, Father?

A book was a heavy and bulking technology, very much like a coffin, for it, too, was a dark space that stored a past. Archivists would share their stories with The Page and a book was The Page's tomb.

But what was contained *in the book? How was the story expressed? Now we use our voices and our bodies, but how was the story told?*

The fathers would smile at their girls, admiring their quizzical natures. *The story was relayed through symbols that lived on The Page. Archivists would let a thought loiter in their head and then, when it could loiter no longer because the archivist was overcome with the story like a fever in break, it was recorded in code. The book would travel long distances from the archivist so that those far as well as near could discern meaning by decoding it. This is what we mean when we say the people of long ago* read. *The reader was a kind of monster, entering the psyche of the characters in order to consume the tale.* And because the daughters knew that a monster was, essentially, a threat, they did not want to hear more.

But what of the archivist?

The archivist became a ghost.

The daughters would tilt their heads. *What is a ghost?*

A very sophisticated shadow. The girls would think then, being a ghost is better than being a monster. *This is one of the reasons books were deemed so dangerous and paper was outlawed; people could no longer determine the line between reality and artifice.*

The girls would nod their heads very quickly to indicate they understood, sitting with their elbows on the counter or the table, or propped up on the bed, palms cradling their chins.

Then they would ask, *Tell of the shadow maidens and their fathers*, and the men would smile widely and lightly tap an index finger to the tip of their daughters' nose.

How about this: next week we will visit the Museum of Paternal Understanding and let the exhibits tell the shadow maidens' tales.

What they knew but did not say is that the stories of the shadow maidens ended in palatable ways, while the ice girl's story did not. This is why the shadow maidens were better known; their tales were lessons to remember, while the ice girl's fate was a story to forget.

The girls would smile and their fathers would lean over and push aside a bang or tame a wild strand or fix a curly lock that was going the wrong direction. *You know, of course, this all took place long, long ago, in a time when children shed their teeth.*

What do you mean?

Long ago, young children shed a row of teeth before a new row surfaced. For a brief time when they were young they looked very old, their mouths like wounds with bare red gums. Then a new set would crop up, like flowers in the spring.

This would happen every year?

Oh, no, this was only once, the fathers would say, locking the front door. *This happened only once, at the age when children were just learning how to be alone.*

And the fathers would think, This is your age. The fathers would think but not say, You would be losing teeth now.

Much later, when they sit in a circle in the large room on the thirty-third floor of the umbrella factory, the fathers will recall this moment and think they were wrong. Everyone knows daughters are born alone.

MARY AND HER FATHER

It CAN BE ARGUED that every story starts with a monster. But, too, every child begins as a monster—two beings fuse to create a third who is cultivated under the skin until it splits her open to emerge. Or, in the case of the narrative Mary later told, a being can be crafted from the parts of others, sutured together and animated by outside forces. However a body becomes, that becoming is always characterized as monstrous, for the act and art of making is a dark and eerie task.

The girl was born with a visage that was blurry, as though she could only be viewed through tearing eyes. Her father thought she looked as if she had been washed with fire, and what remained was a sea of skin that created gentle waves over her bones. There were breaks here and there for her nose to breathe, her eyes to see, her mouth to speak. But where they lived on the plane of her face and how they operated seemed a logic unfamiliar to him.

She grew and in growing learned about the world and herself—where they intersected and where they did not. She would spend her days inside, studying the inky symbols in the books her father owned. This is how, before she could read, she began to recreate the letters with a tilted pen, flourishing the print with her private ornamentation, garnishing the lines of text with embellished eloquence.

And though her father viewed the letters she created, he never really looked; he only understood that she spent her time alone. As the years developed and the door to her room stayed closed, he grew certain her seclusion meant she knew her face was feared.

On the eve of the girl's twelfth birthday, he presented her with a gift. But when he pulled it from behind his back, she did not understand. And because Mary's father had told her that the way her tongue lived in her ill-formed mouth made her voice sound hollow and wet like the voice of an ancient cave, she said nothing.

He placed the gift on the bed and exited the room, leaving the door cracked a bit. As his daughter moved to shut it, she thought this: is a girl's room a safe, where a father secures he most precious equipment? Or a cage where he ensures it can never escape?

The next morning, when he entered her room to rouse her for the day, he was first taken aback by the way her form was flattened in the bed, her eyes bright white and wide open in her sleep. But as he grew closer, he realized it wasn't her at all, only the gift on her pillow—the mask in place of her head. On the floor lay a note, which he read with a sharp kind of horror that only a father feels. In the most elegant and sublime handwriting he had ever witnessed, curling and coiling around the page and hemmed by a floral border, so that it looked like the text on the stone above a grave, he read:

Beware; for I am fearless, and therefore powerful.

When he read her book years later, he would not know it was she who had written it, for she'd used a man's name. He would find it on his doorstep one morning in the autumn, the time of year she liked best. He would wonder who sent it his direction only briefly, for he was quickly caught in the gears of her story, which disturbed him in the best way.

And though it would haunt him he would read it again and again, feeling there was something just under the surface that was both familiar and foreign, the way your voice grows less like yours as it echoes in a wood or the way a mirror reflects you in reverse. The way the human face is mimicked in a mask.

How did you two meet?, Woodsman asks Wainwright and Angler, takes a sip of his coffee and wipes his palm along his thighs. It is late morning and the men move about the room, conversing with those next to whom they rarely sit. Because it is Daughter's Day, the goal is to do nothing other than pass the time.

Angler looks at Wainwright, who is sitting sideways on his chair. *You tell*, Wainwright says. *It feels more like your story than mine.*

Angler lets his chin fall to his chest, then grabs Wainwright's hand, squeezes it twice. *My wife had grown ill and passed on, and my daughter was in her color phase*, Angler says. *I was about to leave for a long trip—I am a sushi chef and travel a lot—and Wainwright— Wainwright's a mechanic, but you knew that, right?—he was head-lost under the hood of a car when we passed him downtown. He had this amazing scarf on—that damn scarf—and my daughter was mesmerized because she could not find a word for the color. Things were really raw for me then, and my daughter and Wainwright just clicked. He gave her the scarf and then pulled her into his arms—greasy uniform and sweat and grime and all—and told her about the intricate world under the hood of that car. It was the first time I'd heard her laugh since her mother*—here Angler takes a moment to collect himself. *And then Wainwright looked at me with this smile that broke me. And my daughter asked him over for dinner and then he took me to bed.* Angler squeezes Wainwright's hand once more, then releases his grip. When he speaks, his voice is lower. *Really I had little to say in the matter. It was more an affair between them.*

Wainwright mouths to Woodsman, *Daughter's Day,* and Woodsman nods back.

Outside, the bells chime noon.

THIS IS HOW THE stories used to look:

Every woman was once a girl,
and every girl was once a daughter.
For every woman in the world
there will always be laughter in slaughter.

Now the stories look like this:

There will always be laughter in slaughter.

WHY DID THE ICE girl not speak? the girls would ask, looking up from the sand at the park or from a puzzle in the kitchen, looking in the mirror at the father who stood behind them as they brushed their hair before bed.

The fathers would tilt their heads and admire their curious girls. *She was frightened of the changes taking place in her body. She was frightened that she had brought them on herself.*

So she chose.

Yes. It was not a sentencing. It was a decision.

The girls would grow solemn, thinking, and the fathers would look up at the sky or the ceiling, imagining. Then the girls would interrupt them in hushed tones: *What is frightening about this story is that it could be real.*

The fathers would grow very solemn. *Nonsense,* the fathers would say, turning their daughters to look at them. *This was in a time so long ago, the stories are fully myth. It was so long ago that our bodies were radically different. For example, this takes place in a time when our fingernails had to be sheared. Our fingernails used to grow very long and they needed to be trimmed in order to keep them from overwhelming our hands.*

But they don't bother us now.

This is because the nails, like the lashes of your eyes, just naturally stop growing when they realize they are long enough. You must remember, the fathers would tell their daughters, *this was in a time when the body was not quite finished evolving. Back then, there was an understanding that the body could be labeled as having all kinds of conditions if it was somehow out of order. This is what happens in the stories of the shadow maidens; their fathers deemed them failed and ill and wrong.*

But Father, the girls would press, *I don't understand. In what order should the body be?*

THE POINT IS NOT to forget them, but just to remember less. They know without the meetings they, too, would be lost, a group of lost boys missing the echo of their girls.

And sometimes, usually at the meetings held at night, the men with daughters who are Alices—Barber, Smith, Wainwright, Angler—break off to talk about the women those girls would make. These phantom women mimic the moves of the men with missing girls as they navigate town; the women who look twice at the men in the bar or who make quick smiles at the bus stop—the women who slide shyly by in the grocery store.

That could be my daughter, they say. I saw a woman who could be. I saw a woman—daughter. A woman who could be—did I see my daughter? I saw a woman: Daughter. Who could be, that could be my daughter. A woman who could be. A daughter. Mine.

A WOMAN IS A catalyst for chaos. Proof lives in the territory women occupy and then abandon. For examples of such territory, see a father's heart.

The women their girls were to become live in the cleft between fiction and fact. To conjure them requires suspended disbelief. This is how the men with missing daughters can think of them in safe, clean ways.

For here lies the locus of guilt: fatherhood is about control. The governing father has failed when the domestic ties untether.

As the men imagine the women their girls were to become, they learn to swallow malice. Because while the past *can* haunt, the future always does.

After a daughter exits, most movement hurts. This is because the daughter-father paradigm mutates. It starts as a thick cord pulled taut with no slack. Then the cord splits into many lines and the lines extend and fold around each other to create a net in which both are caught. When daughter-exit occurs, the net dissolves, leaving the father free to be haunted by the ghost of his girl.

When the men speak of the women their girls were to become, their conversation launches open-ended questions that are never resolved.

For example: At what point in the lifespan of a woman does her identity as daughter end?

For example: Was the notion of the daughter invented or discovered?

For example: Are fathers born or bred?

When another person takes your daughter—either abducting her alive and toward an unknown, or ending her life, her womanhood amputated—the limits of the possible collapse. Your world becomes a woman you will never know, who loiters spectral in the places where you are most vulnerable: coming out of the shower, or with the dust of thirst in your mouth, alone at night in the bad parts of the city. Put simply, it is a loss equal to a forfeited tongue. It is a loss like the loss of the knowledge that one thing plus another makes two.

In short, when the men want to summarize the women their girls were to become through theory, it comes out something like this: without horizon, a landscape portrait from very far away is just a map.

DAUGHTERS FEEL MOST GONE in the morning. There is no young form to climb into bed to wake fathers from slumber, no breakfast to prepare or pajamas to lift over a soft head. There is no hair to braid, no shoes to tie. There are no teeth to brush.

But why did the ice girl have shadow maidens? the girls would ask, in line at the market or walking down the street, raking leaves or watering the plants.

The ice girl lived a lonely life and so she invented friends.

What about her father?

Her father had important business in the World of Thought and Books.

Where was the World of Thought and Books?

It was transposed over the ice girl's home, the same way you are sometimes a daughter and sometimes a friend and all the time both, though one stays dormant when the other is called on.

What's doormat?

Dormant, dear child. Dormant. It means concealed, like the place inside you from which your tears come, the men would say, picking up their girls and securing them on their hips. *But this was so long ago! This was long, long ago, in the time when women still bled.*

But women bleed now, the girls would say. *I have seen cuts on the fingers of ladies.*

This is true. But women also used to bleed regularly from the place where their legs meet. For several days a year, following a pattern that related to the moon and the way the sea behaved.

The girls allowed this to sink in. They were just starting to understand that the mysterious occupation known as womanhood lurked at the end of their own narratives. *Why did they bleed?* the girls would finally ask.

Because the place where their legs meet was thought to be a wound, the fathers would say. *Now, of course, we know it as a device.*

THIS IS HOW FATHERS imagine their daughters understand the relationship between the past and the future:

This is how daughters really think:

CHARLOTTE AND HER FATHER

THERE ARE SOME STORIES that do not work toward cataclysm but open in the midst of it. Whether that story begins with a discarded wife locked in an attic or a mother kept in a room with yellowed walls, the story opens at a precipice. This is how some stories—from the initial word—are all about descent.

Charlotte was born and raised in a house behind which lay a graveyard for the patients her father could not save. As a result, her life revolved around The End and was therefore cloaked in mourning, a heavy, evolving sadness that materialized in unexpected ways.

For years she coped with what her father called her illness of the head. Medicine was his practice, and because he had treated several other girls, he thought he knew the best methods for making her well. The most successful had been to place a girl in a room and shut the door and go away.

One day her father informed her he was to be gone for several weeks. He pulled her covers up to her chin and kissed the places where her bangs met her brows. Before he left the room, he turned around and requested that she smile. She obliged him, but when his back was to her, the smile faded quickly. She thought this: which is more dangerous—a door, through which one can only imagine what lies beyond, or a window, which exposes its possibility like a baited lure?

Because women have a history of being tended to like a sculpture made of already cracked and failing glass, they also have a history of defying. As soon as the house was empty of him, Charlotte wrapped herself in coats and left to walk the city. There she came upon the town's Language Museum, a building saturated in books, those mysterious devices that allowed one to exit the world in which one's body moved and enter a plurality of others.

For the fortnight he was gone, she removed books from the Language Museum for no cost at all, only the promise that she would return them. And by the time her father returned, she had realized the antidote to her strife—that the way to quell her illness was not through carefully curated passivity, but through rigorous thought.

When her father returned a day early, on the eve of her twelfth birthday, and, in the hopes of surprising her, swung open the door to her room without knocking, what he witnessed was a sight for which he was unprepared. There was his daughter—his offspring and his patient, both; his charge and his work—eagerly consuming the conduit for that risky enterprise known as contemplation.

The next morning, her father made a deal with the Manager of the Language Museum, that he would donate copies of his most rare texts if the Manager promised not to lend his daughter any more books. And when next she snuck away and pulled open the grand doors of the Language Museum, the Manager shook his head and pushed her back and locked her out.

Now her desolation took new shape, for she knew what would quell it, but was forbidden access to the corrective. Now her sadness meant walking into swift rivers with the aim of not walking out, going barefoot into woods hoping never to be found. Now her sadness meant screaming the opening lines to her favorite books while she hung naked from trees in the yard.

The morning he came to tell her he would place her in the Home for the Harmed, he put his ear to the door and heard laughter. And as he twisted the knob, his stomach sank. For he felt and then saw that she was gone, the window dressing moving in the breeze. The laughing was coming from the sound machine—she must have recorded herself.

Years later, he would find her books at the Language Museum, though he would never know the words were hers, for they bore men's names. And—reading with a physician's eye—he would think these narratives were those of a sick man. The books contained the stories of women who were abandoned—in an attic while her husband fell in love with an orphaned governess below, or in a room with bars, the acrid, amber wallpaper teasing her. He would think the work powerful but failed because it contained such aggression. Yet he found himself irresistibly drawn, compelled, in fact, to reading such dim and lurid tales. It was on these evenings, after reading the stories he could not know were born under his roof, that he would draw closed the drapes, synch the sound machine, and drain a glass of liquor, listening to the fractured record of his little girl's laugh.

As the men wait on the thirty-third floor for their leader to arrive, they watch the city from the wide window. Butcher refills the tray of biscuits and puts on another pot of coffee before he joins the others, already entering debate.

Maybe he's prepared to move on. Or maybe it has to do with the secret of his daughter.

The men sit back in their chairs as they contemplate this theory.

Woodsman says, leaning in, *We have waited to hear his narrative for years. We do not even know his last name. It could be that his daughter's story has shifted or is changed. We should be prepared to be supportive, however that support takes shape.*

Sometimes they get mad at their girls. Sometimes their voices grow loud. When the men try to point to the element that most angers them, it is the threat of wonder and marvel that makes girls curious.

It is a paradox, they know, as curiosity is the method by which we gain knowledge through the hazardous realm of investigating the unfamiliar. Generally speaking, this means quaint adventures and structured escapades. But once in a while, girls venture toward territory they do not know without instrument or acquaintance. And it is then that girls chance getting lost.

For the fathers, this means avoiding curiosity. And for the FOLD in particular, this means not asking about Peter's girl. For they have learned the hard way that knowledge must be managed or else it will destroy.

WHAT PETER THINKS BUT cannot come to say:

That his daughter left daughterhood behind.

That he started the FOLD to cope with the isolation that defines a fatherhood of radical loss, no matter how that loss takes shape, whether in the known world or in the contours of the father psyche.

That he is ashamed. That he is ashamed to reveal his particular form of daughter loss because he lost only one iteration of his daughter, not the flesh being.

That the truth in its completeness is this: Peter's daughter is now his son.

How do we know the story of the ice girl? the girls would ask, between bites or pulling on their boots, folding back the covers of the bed.

I'm not sure what you mean.

From where did the story come?

It was passed through mouths and hands and performances from people of one set of years to the next until it exited my mouth en route to fill yours.

But Father, the girls would say, *who told you?*

And here the fathers would pause. They would take a moment to think, scratching their beards or scrunching their brows, tapping fingers to lips. *To tell you the truth, I don't remember. It is a tale so woven into the fabric of our world that it feels as though the story has always lived.*

The girls will contemplate what this means. *Who will I tell?*

My dear, the fathers would say, picking up their girls to get a closer look at them. *Our stories are told to teach. You will one day care about someone enough to relay this story.*

But aren't our stories told to entertain?

That was true once upon a time, but that was long ago.

But Father, why must I tell someone I care about? Why could I not tell someone who has hurt me or with whom I am angry? Why could I not tell a stranger? Shouldn't we also teach people who are full of vice and malice? Shouldn't we be teaching them most of all?

The fathers would look at the ceiling or out the window; the fathers would look at the floor. *I love you very much*, the fathers would say, holding their girls tightly, *and I hope you will respect me when I say that you have asked plenty of questions for today.*

WHILE THE MEN WHOSE daughters are missing speculate on where they are now, the men who father Dorothies—Miller, Woodsman, Butcher, Baker—do not have the luxury of imagining the terrain of elsewhere their girls navigate. When the men whose girls are missing break off, the men whose girls are dead are left only with the sad and ugly task of chronicling where and when their daughters are not. Where and when and how and why their daughters are not. Where, when, how, why, and also what. What their daughters are not.

A DAUGHTER IS NOT dark clouds on a winter day.

A daughter is not the quilt that covers sick legs, a spoiled celebration.

A daughter is not a minor chord, nor the rope binding a pair of struggling feet.

A daughter is not an abandoned cup of tea gone cold, nor the paper links of a chain made by hands now grave.

A daughter is not an undeveloped photograph, nor the broken leg of an antique chair.

A daughter is not the spice rack, nor the sugar bowl, the driveway that ends before it meets the road.

A daughter is not a frail and failing sweater, the cracking paint on a wall behind which dark tasks are undertaken.

A daughter is not hot milk, nor the pavement, nor what we have come to understand as adventure.

A daughter is not a brave sun that dares to rise the morning after an important death, the craters of the moon or the stings of a wasp.

A daughter is not a weather catastrophe, fruit, or music.

A daughter is not a knife, nor a fingernail clipping; a daughter is not a satchel, nor a damp pair of underwear, nor a cutting board.

A daughter is not the stairs that lead to the cellar, nor your debt.

A daughter is not the lesson that less is more.

A daughter is not the act of winding, the wind, a healing wound or coils of wire wound round a neck.

A daughter is not a vehicle, soft glass, tomorrow.

A daughter is not gravity, nor the drawing of the blinds.

A daughter is not a son.

> In a dark hollow in a wood at twilight, a daughter that was is not.

BY THE TIME THE clock chimes three, the men are occupying themselves with tales about the day they learned their daughters were going to be born. They discuss the moment they found out and how their elation was followed by daunting fear.

Then the men speak of learning the babies inside the bellies of the women who were going to be mothers would be girls.

At first it is a kind of relief—the child will not have to go through boyhood. The child will be relieved of the struggles that accompany being a boy-child in this world.

This brief reprieve is followed by a sinking revelation, which is this: their daughters will live lives they cannot know. Because daughters are vague and haunted, complex devices that must be maintained.

Eventually, the men break for their only meal of the day. Today—as on every Daughter's Day—the men have packed their lunches in memory of their girls. Quietly they pull out their daughters' favorite meals.

Outside, the bells chime five and the men think not *when* will Peter come, but *will* he?

What Peter thinks but cannot come to say:

That though he does not know what it is like to experience a child who's passed on or is missing, to witness a child engaged in long-term suffering is to be at the bottom of what he imagines to be an equally deep abyss.

That it started through mentions of feeling misplaced and a request that he call his child *son*. That at first Peter thought it had to do with imagination and play. But as the insistence moved outside of the safe realm of theater at home and into the public sphere, Peter realized this desire to be called a boy-child was not a byproduct of make-believe. And this is when Peter began to feel in the core of his father-being that the dialogues were no longer in service of creating an environment for play. The performance grew ever more convincing, more deliberate, until a day came when it was made clear that this was not a role cast but a life craved.

That at first Peter thought a child this size could not know the scope or scale of Life to Come. That the more Peter tried to tell himself that this was the thrill and enchantment characteristic of childhood wishing, the more he could not determine where his child's performance ended and identity began.

That eventually his minute child, the offspring raised by his own hand, had used the word *intolerable* to describe the situation. That his thoughts went immediately not toward the statement itself but toward the effort the child must have put into learning the word. That his child had said, standing in the kitchen wearing only a pair of boy-child underwear, arms crossed and eyes closed tight, *This is intolerable*. Peter interpreted this not as a threat, but a foreshadowing, an omen. And so, both languidly haunted and nudged into action by what this statement meant, events began to unfold.

That he looked for others who shared his story in the Archive of Narrative. That he sought out every brand of storyteller and every genre of tale—the true and the not, the ethereal and the concrete, the particular and the universal—in order to learn if his narrative was shared. That he had never experienced such visceral loneliness as the realization that these narratives were so few.

That to wrap the tongue around the *he* was perhaps the hardest part. That this was hardest because it meant revising the architecture of the father mind, recasting a then-familiar body into another role. It meant abandoning a certain kind of logic in search of a healthier one. In the end, it required a gentle and strategic recalibration to understand and recognize that a square is not a circle, nor a circle a square, but that—if you care to look hard enough—they are not in opposition. Rather, both live on the same plane of shape.

That his son requested he place a coin in the word jar not when he swore, but when he said *she* or *her*. That he practiced, in all kinds of glass—both in public and wherever he faced it at home. That he watched his reflection tell him over again for months, "I am the father of a son." That at first it felt like a splitting and then a failed suturing, but he knew it had to be done. For if it did not start with the father, where would it begin?

That Peter's union with the child's mother dissolved when she would not accept their child's Shift. That it started with lengthier eras of absence until he found her away for days. That when he asked her about her distance, her mouth and mind stayed fused shut.

That when finally she left for real and always, she asked why the child was doing this to her. *Try*, he would tell her. *I* she would say back, over and over: *Me*. That in the end, she believed the Shift was not their child's personal, local desire, but an external gesture of malevolence.

That in the beginning Peter, too, thought about himself—that perhaps he was at fault, had somehow launched through his own body's chemistry the internal events that caused his child's Body-Spirit Synthesis Disorder. That he could not let go of the idea that he'd done something wrong in that twilight world of two-human union. That in the end this assumption placed at the center of the situation not the child but himself.

That the allegory of the ice girl and her father without risks serves to inform us that parents who choose not to explain the world to their children are dangerous.

That the moral of his own narrative serves to inform us that parents who choose not to listen to their children explaining the world to them are more dangerous still.

That there was only one way to safely escape the complex web he faced, and that was this: sanction and implement his own daughter-loss to welcome, in her place, his son.

THERE ARE SOME STORIES that linger on the periphery of the mind. There are some stories that make the nature of telling a complicated web of deceit, for while stories told over and over become reduced and calcified, they are also misheard and sometimes confused with other tales. And sometimes the tales are purposefully manipulated such that the dark parts that might induce heavy feelings go untold.

Why did the people of once long ago not tell stories aloud? Why did they tell them to The Page? their daughters would ask, usually in autumn, for autumn is the season of girls.

The fathers would look at their girls with a jealous kind of longing, admiring their desire to know. *The Page was the conduit for distributing story. It was the way a single tale could be accessed by several thinkers in different places all at once. One could train The Page to do what one needed it to do. For example, it could make one cry.*

But if it was just a bit of paper, a layer of dangerous tree lace with symbols, how did this occur?

An excellent question, the fathers would say, and gently pinch their chins. *The symbols held a certain kind of power that could make one forget. This was how The Page would trick one into believing certain events had actually come to pass.*

Just as the fathers began to think of other things, the girls would ask: *How does the ice girl's story end?*

The fathers would look directly into their eyes. The fathers would recall the first time they held their daughters, and they would think of how the daughter body releases the soft smell of heat. *The end can't be revealed until you're older.*

The daughters would not object. Because the fathers told them when they were very young that time is a factory and age the product of the factory's toil. So the daughters knew as small children that wishing to grow up swiftly was a venture as senseless as hoping for a weatherless day.

The girls would reach for their fathers' hands, thinking silently that they were glad they were born after The Touch Wars.

VIRGINIA AND HER FATHER

EVERY STORY IS PURSUED by its own end. As in life, the characters do not know their fate. But the narrator knows how the story will end from the moment she begins.

Virginia was born in the shadow of her sister, whom she loved very much. They were close in a way only sisters who have endured sorrow can be. Their mother had died of a then-common disease of the chest flesh that often afflicted women. The night they lost their mother, Virginia and her sister walked to the wood, lit a thick candle, and promised that they would stay forever bound. As everyone knows, women who experience certain kinds of horror and harm overcome it by suturing their lives together.

In those first years without their mother, Virginia's sister decided she was meant to be a performer. Virginia walked with her to rehearsals in the city and sat at the back of the theatre, where she had the whole performance to herself. She watched her sibling portray other women, and while she recognized that the form in front of her was her sister, she also knew it was, by some kink in the plane of logic, not. From the plush seats, her hands growing damp from anticipation in the moment before her sister stepped from behind the curtain and into sight, Virginia found herself falling for the trick. She felt she loved not just her sister, but also each and every woman that her sister captured and performed. She felt it in the core of her bones and the channels of her blood, the places where her mother had said true feeling is born.

While Virginia admired her sister's chosen field, she herself preferred the careful folding of paper. She had always found the properties of paper captivating because of its role as both artifact and conduit. Because her mother had studied this craft, too, she used her mother's work as a guide, unfolding each creation to examine the ways the paper pleated and caved. She started with still figures: a rock, a pond, a tree. Then she moved on to more intricate scenes—a field with an abandoned bathtub, a row of empty and disheveled beds lying on a basement floor—and finally to full narratives. She would fold a story and present it to her father, and each time he read her paper stories, he would nod in gratitude, then gently kiss the top of her head. For through this artifice Virginia was resurrecting for him the woman they'd both lost.

Virginia's sister grew to be such a fine actress that she left to pursue her art in the region's largest cities. Virginia stayed at home, and at night she would think of the myriad of women her sister was embodying, a myriad of women her sister was not. At first she believed it was because she so desperately missed her sister and wanted to find sisterhood through them. But she thought of them in ways that were more secretive than kinship. And as the other youth in the city began to speak of that mysterious attraction we deem love, she decided this was the abstract allure she felt.

Because daughterhood requires long periods of being alone, Virginia often visited the river to conduct her folding. On one such day, she came upon a pair of women who were tangled together on the grass. At first she thought they were fighting, but when she moved around the trees to chance a better view, she came to understand that they were kissing. While she realized this was something ambiguous and intangible, something she could not fully unpack, she also realized the tingling in her bones and blood that said one day she would lie with a woman, too. It was something far less than desire but more than mere interest; it was something akin to appeal.

Soon Virginia found her room was full of the story of women loving each other, paper narratives told in the dialect of girl. In this way, her room became a stage, and on it, her imagination was given permission to be made real.

On the eve of her twelfth birthday, her father knocked on her door. Detecting no response, he entered but found the room empty of daughter, full only of the sound of paper speaking in the breeze. He looked around, first in adoration and then in an effort to relive the days when his wife would fold him stories. But as he consumed Virginia's narrative, knowledge slowly percolated in his mind. He read and reread; he read in all directions. He was a careful reader of folded stories, having learned the craft from his late wife. And this is how his daughter's message was made clear.

Virginia came home that evening balancing several reams of paper. As she entered the house, she saw in her father's eyes a kind of fear and defeat that told her to put the reams down.

You thirst for girls, he said. And she looked into his eyes and smiled, for there it was—it had been said aloud—and she felt unsheathed, as though an invisible robe that had been holding her arms across her chest was unfastened and, after a lifetime without them, she could finally use her hands.

She told him then that it was true and not to worry, for love between women is the safest kind. But her father did not understand. How would she carry on a family? How would she create children within her frame?

Virginia told her father then that not all families contain children. She had no intention of ever mothering, for, as she had recently been thinking, she was not sure what children were. Were they the way a person ensured something was left crawling and creeping on earth's soil when she was buried? Were they the shadowy apparitions of all the people of her lineage? Were they a kind of self-centered pleasure or a kind of self-induced pain? Put less simply, were children the rubric or the body of work?

Virginia was still awake hours later, when her father returned from a long walk around the village. He was quiet for a long while, and Virginia listened, wondering if a daughter chose to be one, or was sentenced upon birth. Daughterhood is a vocation concerned with following carefully prescribed rules, avoiding endangerment, evading threat; being a daughter means mastering the art of defense. The wonder, then, is what would happen to a daughter who rebelled.

What Virginia did not know then but would soon learn is this: anything could happen when daughterhood ceased to be a protected occupation.

Virginia crept from her room.

It had taken him several drafts, but there it lay; the story of what was to become of Virginia, written in a missive to her sister. She read it with a kind of horror and confusion, a kind of disgusted awe. For her mother had taught her that love was rare and when it surfaced, it should be invited very gently into one's life. Love, her mother had said, was like the thinnest paper; easily torn but capable of the largest number of folds.

Before she left, she placed two folded words upon her bedroom door. *For You*, a dedication for the paper story her room told. For a room is like a book, in that it is a private province. A room is like a book in that it is most charged with possibility when it is entered alone.

When Virginia's sister would go on stage to perform the women she was not, she imagined Virginia might be out there in the audience. She hoped that if she were, Virginia would see in her movements that freedom is not a state but a dwelling, a room one of one's own. And when her sister found a narrative couched between the covers of a book written by Anonymous, she read Virginia in the margins of the story—she read what was left unsaid.

From the stage, an audience looks like a single being that moves uniformly in laughter or through tears, taken aback or pulled in. The players on stage are a cast of apparitions who mimic and mirror the failures and follies of the many-mouthed beast. Virginia's sister would think this as she took her place in the dark of backstage for her curtain call. As the curtains rose and the lights shone, she would lift her lips into that faux, required smile and the audience would howl and clap and stand. And there, toward the back, would be always her father. He would stop clapping then and leave before being seen, as he was now estranged to both of his daughters. But it was in these moments he came to understand the first rule of narrative: if you break it down and apart, in the end, every story is about a woman and her machine.

AT SUNDOWN THE MEN recite their mantra twice and listen to a fresh pot of coffee brewing. The sun goes down over the city, swelling the closer it gets to the horizon, which they watch from the massive windows on the west side of the thirty-third floor of the abandoned umbrella factory.

The evening ritual involves silent reflection on the events of the day she became lost. In one of the first years, they had gone around the circle to tell the whole story, but this was a grave mistake. The first to go—Barber—had barely finished his tale when several members broke down. Butcher kept repeating that he could not do it, and by the time it was Woodsman and then Smith's turn, they realized the horror of the thing they had done; they had mandated a reliving. And because the men were vehement in rules regarding uniformity, their act now required every man in the group to tell his tale. The subsequent meeting made it clear that this event was the closest to catastrophe the group had ever been. Moving forward, the Daughter's Day procedure would adopt silence after the sun went down to commemorate her life, not her loss.

As hours pass and the day reduces, they grow increasingly anxious that Peter may not come. It is crawling toward night and the men are full of coffee and regret.

As the silence hovers in the room, the men think of the last few conversations they had with their daughters. How those conversations had been populated with questions about the veracity of story.

I know the story is not real, but Father, the girls said, *is the story true? The story of the ice girl and her father without whisks?*

Risks, the fathers would say, *her father without risks. And yes, for all stories that feel dimensionless are true. All stories that are amplified infinitely are true, and it is at the very center of the tale where lies The Truth.*

But now, on the thirty-third floor of the umbrella factory at the end of Daughter's Day, the men think their reply was fallacious. Now, as they watch the sun sink behind the cityscape, they think this: the story of the ice girl and her father without risks cannot be true, because risks are everywhere, always, living at the break of day, at the moment before the body decides to wake.

But more to the point, the story is not true, the men think, watching the sun turn the city into an open wound, because stories that feel dimensionless and that are infinitely amplified are neither fact nor fiction, but tucked firmly in the fissure between. These stories live neither in the Lands of Never nor the Land of Now. These stories live in the Region of Perhaps.

WHAT PETER THINKS BUT cannot come to say:

That he thinks of his son's birth as a series of vignettes: cropped hair, skinned knees, bad words.

That he thinks of his daughter as spectral.

That the period between son and daughterhood was marked by tumultuous events: regular visits to the Thought Doctor to diagnose him with Body-Spirit Synthesis Disorder; quarterly visits to the Corporeal Fluid Authorities to get permission for male serum; three visits to the Governing Order to legally change the child's name; too-often visits from the Law Keepers, the collateral damage of a childhood characterized by the urgency to amend.

That time became an obstacle: get his name changed before schooling, get his body fluid levels right before multiversity, get him through another Child-to-Adult Change before the first is done.

That he cannot remember how many times he asked his child, *Are you sure?* That he knows now each time he asked it, the question hurt his son.

That he cringed when they called his child *disordered*—that it was required to move forward with the Shift, but that he prefers to think of his child as exercising Body-Spirit creativity.

That there were years of visiting Thought Doctors in an effort to get him diagnosed. That his child disdained such visits because they made the child lay bare his every thought in order to secure permission for the medical aspects of the Shift. That in the end, they decided that the child's desires were "valid." That in the end they told him that his child's desires were "real."

That they had to discuss two-human union far earlier than he would have ever thought because it affected the decision to give him scheduled shots of male serum. That they had to discuss the possibility of his child bearing children, should events unfold unconventionally.

That all the Corporeal Fluid Authorities could offer as they reviewed the risks was *may cause* and *could lead to* and *possibly induce*. That the Corporeal Fluid Authorities consistently told them society needed more trustworthy research to be sure of the long-term effects.

That in those moments, Peter could think only that his story must not be unique, and if he could swing his story from the margins of society to the center, perhaps his son would not have to deal with such serious uncertainty.

That despite the risks, they moved forward because they could comprehend no another way. That this uncertainty now haunts them quietly, privately.

That his child never truly had a childhood because it was riddled with efforts to maneuver who he'd be as an adult. That on the way home from the regular trips to the Thought Doctors, the child would talk about the future as an abstract ever-after and the present as a means toward getting there.

That he worries for his child's safety and security every day, worries about reactions from those with closed minds. How the horror of violence hovers above the hours they spend apart and ceases only when his child walks through his door.

That he knows his son endures forms of prejudgment, but that his son has learned to carefully disregard this. When he thinks of his son at night, as he is falling asleep, his thoughts toggle between pride and protection.

That if he had not interceded—financially, emotionally—the risks would hang heavy in his mind: abuse of substances, introduction of viruses, living without a home, or even end-of-life self-initiation. Conscious of the ways he did not let events unfold, he is thankful for each morning his son hugs him.

That to be born with and abide by Body-Spirit Synthesis is a privilege. That if this is you, you are lucky. That if this is you, you are blessed.

That one day in the future, his story will be languaged and dispersed because children whose spirits desire a Body Shift will be as commonplace and ubiquitous as the fact that men rule the domestic and women leave home to work.

That it is time to speak what Peter thinks but so far has not come to say.

That because we have so few stories about such children in the Archive of Narrative, Peter will tell his.

It is night and the men are preparing to gather their coats. Just as they are rising to fold their chairs, they hear a knock. Woodsman turns toward the room's door but Smith grabs his arm. *We left the door open*, he says, and Woodsman replies, *I know*. With the knock on the door, the fact is made clear: to enter, Peter is asking permission.

Woodsman greets him with a nod and a cup of coffee. Peter takes the cup and holds it with two hands, then raises it to his lips for a cautious sip. He sits at the head of the circle and meets the gaze of every other man. Then he nods his head and begins.

EVERY DAUGHTER WAS ONCE a girl, except his.

It started with shadow. The child Peter then called *she* would watch it for hours, casting her form on the ground. Something about it was wrong. She used to tell him it wasn't hers and a cold chill would run down his spine. She would say it wasn't hers and then point to the place where her form ended and her shadow began. *See the gap?* she would say. *It is not connected. This one isn't mine.*

This was when she was two. And this is how he came to know that two is the beginning of the end.

The Lands of Never are not some mythic district; they are the places you think you will not ever be. But he found himself there, in the Lands of Never, when he inserted the needle into her thigh that introduced to her body the serum that would make her male, and held her hand after the surgery to remove her breasts. When he saw hair growing on the chin of what he still thought of as his daughter. When the voice dropped to a baritone and his child started smiling again.

So imagine girls with ribbons, dolls, and bracelets; building blocks and dirty nails and mussed bangs. And then imagine his: his, who could not look in a mirror, who never slept. His, who was so disgusted by the sight of herself naked that in the middle of her fourth year she stopped bathing.

What changed his mind was the day she looked up at him and held up a handful of hair. *My hair, it's falling out,* she said, and it was; it was falling out at a frightening rate. Later they told him it was because of stress. *Does this mean it's time?* She was so full to the brim with promise. *Time for what?* her father asked. *My real body. The body I'm supposed to have. I must be shedding this one so the real one can come through.*

Peter started the FOLD to grow free of his daughter. Because he had a daughter once, too. And while he is now the happy father of a healthy son, he still thinks about the past.

This is how he is the father of a daughter who he never saw grow up. He is the father of a daughter who is lost. But his loss is different, and he knows there are others who understand her particular brand of gone. That is how the FOLD started, and that is how he will start another group for the Parents of Once-Daughters-Now-Sons.

FATHERHOOD IS AN INDUSTRY and a daughter is a beach. But what binds them is cycle and scope. You can put the contracts in your briefcase—you can put the shells in your pocket—but you can't bring home the business or the shore.

Peter's full story takes hours to tell, and when it is finally done, the men sit in comfortable silence. Throughout they have been reading each other's bodies, and this is how they know that Peter is at once already gone and will never leave.

They sit suspended for what feels like ages and it becomes a kind of enchantment, this quiet. That the hours pass but the men register only minutes speaks to the slippery something that we call time, which elongates or contracts accordingly. For time is a device founded within the site of the mind. While many have spent whole lives trying to interrogate this invention, what we know without question is this: time was born to allow us to tell our tales.

And as the Fathers of Lost Daughters sit in this ebbing temporal site, morning breaches the cityscape and begins to slowly fill the thirty-third floor of the abandoned umbrella factory. It first breaks in a bright beam nearest the window and then stretches lazily over the circle of men, reaching the bottom apex of the circle and then growing north; at first it touches Miller and Smith, then Wainwright and Woodsman. Angler and Butcher are next, then Barber and finally, at the peak, Peter himself.

It is after the sun has risen and the men realize they have made it through another Daughter's Day that Barber decides to speak up.

Do you know that cautionary tale about the ice girl and her father without risks? Barber asks.

Yes, that story—I would tell her every night. She wanted to hear it all the time, Butcher says.

Smith chuckles to himself. *It's funny,* he says. *I never wanted to tell her the end because it was so cruel. You know how folklore can be so ugly—I wanted to spare her,* Smith says, and looks up into the rafters of the room. *But I spent so many years leaving off the end that I can't myself remember how it goes.*

I remember, says Angler, grabbing Wainwright's hand.

So do I, says Woodsman, and Barber nods.

I told her I would tell her when she was older, Miller says, seemingly to himself, and Butcher nods, while the other men join in with a chorus of *me too*s.

Would you tell it now? Smith asks. *Please?*

BECAUSE ICE CONTESTS LOGIC, it only follows that the ice girl would transgress. The ice girl placed her work on display and many people came to view it. This is how the ice girl exhibited her fears. And when her father arrived, prepared to bear witness, he always missed that which she aimed to display, as she had committed herself to a medium that, with time, is lost. This is how, even when she began to speak again after her fifth year, she found herself still mute.

In the exhibit that would come to be deemed her last, the ice girl chose a new medium, shifting from an ice girl to a woman of glass. Her father would not miss her final show. As the Laws of Climate tell us, glass is solid when its temperature is equal to that of a room.

And this is how, when he entered the exhibit in the typical manner—late—the father without risks did not see a floor wet with the past, but rather stood witness to her work. The work was this: massive teeth living in half of an oval, opening at the exhibit entrance so that spectators stood in the place where a tongue might rest.

The father's entrance into the work struck him like a blow and he was overcome with emotion. To perceive these transparent masses in their grandeur was enough to resurrect a series of images he never knew, images of his daughter's early projects, of the woman the ice girl never called mother in her final, ugly days. And he thought then of his daughter at age ten and fourteen, at age twenty, sitting alone, the crowd gone, watching the heat devour her work, watching the body of ice she had so carefully managed come under the control of another force, that frightening mechanism called time. For years the father had thought that his daughter's artwork was mere play, but he understood in that moment that what she was doing was everything play is not.

This revelation launched the desire to see her. But when he searched through the exhibition, his daughter could not be found. For she had nestled herself into the tiny back room of the grandiose gallery and, practicing poise, posed herself between two cement blocks among the closet's collection of display ephemera. Then she began to slip fragments of jagged glass across that abstract plane where arm and hand meet.

The shocked cries of those who found her matched perfectly the stunned noise of those who entered the gallery to stand witness to her latest work. The rooms lived on opposite ends of the building, and so the response permeated the space, reverberating off the walls and saturating the confines of the exhibit. Though in reply to two radically different events, the sound was the same: it was the sound of thwarted expectation.

And so the story of the ice girl and her father without risks lacks a transparent, singular lesson, because its lesson is at once amplified and fractured, like a shattered mirror.

But because we are human beings and therefore exercise a longing to translate experience to knowledge that can be passed on, the story might be reduced to this: the opposite of play is not that which is serious, but that which is real.

BEFORE HE LEAVES, THE men ask Peter his surname. Peter tells them, shakes each man's hand, and then walks out the door.

The fathers adjourn the meeting with their mantra. It is as they are saying it together that they realize the first line no longer holds.

> Every woman was once a girl
> and every girl was once a daughter
> For every woman in the world,
> there will always be laughter in slaughter.

The men rise and their chairs make a scraping sound on the floor. They grab their coats and bags, begin to prepare themselves to head toward home. On the way out the door, Butcher says, *Ryder, huh. After all these years. His last name was Ryder.*

No, Barber says, *he said Righter. Righter, or that which is not wrong.*

I heard Writer, Angler says, miming a pen and using his palm as a tablet.

That old, archaic vocation? Wainwright says, slipping his arm into Angler's.

Yes, Writer. That's what I heard, Angler says. Wainwright pulls the door closed behind them.

The room is left empty, except for the chairs that live in a half circle. From far above, in the rafters of the abandoned umbrella factory, the chairs look like rotting teeth on the bottom of a mouth.

ABOUT THE AUTHOR

Lindsey Drager is the author of *The Sorrow Proper*, winner of the 2016 Binghamton University / John Gardner Fiction Award. Originally from Michigan, she is an assistant professor of creative writing at the College of Charleston, where she teaches in the MFA program in fiction.

ACKNOWLEDGMENTS

For material borrowed and reimagined in this book:

L. Frank Baum, Lewis Carroll, J.M. Barrie, Mary Shelley, Charlotte Brontë, Charlotte Perkins Gilman, Virginia Woolf, Sigmund Freud, Alan Watts, George Lakoff and Mark Johnson, Fred Botting, Sharon Horvath.

For all else:
Richard Powers, Ander Monson, Selah Saterstrom, Laird Hunt.
Emily Forland, Michelle Dotter, Guy Intoci.
The Vermont Studio Center.
Ron Drager, Valerie Drager.
Leland Drager.
Allan G. Borst.